Chicken or Beef
My Airline Career
(The funny bits!)

By
Wyndham Deere

First edition, published in 2010 by
Bryn Illtyd Publications

Copyright © Wyndham Deere, 2010

All rights reserved
No part of this publication may be reproduced
or transmitted in any form or by any means,
electronic or mechanical, nor may it be stored
in any information storage and retrieval system
without prior permission from the author.

The right of Wyndham Deere
to be identified as author of this work
has been asserted by him in accordance with
the copyright Designs and Patents Act 1*988*

ISBN 978-0-9865238-0-9

Printed in Canada

*All persons mentioned in this book are non-fictional,
and any resemblance to shady characters the reader may know
is entirely possible
However, to avoid embarrassment and possible recourse to the
legal profession, I have changed many of the names. If the reader
thinks he recognizes himself or others in these pages that is but
conjecture on his part, but all these pages are written in a spirit of
goodwill and fond memories.*

	Page	
Introduction		1
Prologue		2
A New Life		5
Characters		9
A short history of Aeroplane Drivers		13
Flat Hats and more Characters		17
Concessionary Travel		23
"Oh, Island in the Sun"		25
Deadheading is not always dull		28
Strangers in the Night		33
Bathing Interlude		36
A Wing and a Prayer		39
Spring Break - Alpine style		41
Ports of Call		46
A Tale of Canadian Tire		50
Disturbing tales		53
Back to Ireland		58
Portuguese Adventure		63
One advantage of radio silence		73
Caveat Emptor		75
Distant Friends		77
Moving at Ground level		83
Apocrypha from the Sub Continent		87
--------and Mooshrooms!		89
Exotic Cuisine		91

Cock-Ups in the Catering Department 93
Finis and Final thoughts 97

Introduction

Some years ago I completed what was intended to be a light hearted account of my life to the time I left the Royal Air Force. Although I had never intended anything more than a limited readership, I got considerable satisfaction in its completion and subsequent self-publication. It was quite well received, and I was occasionally asked when the sequel was coming out.

Whereas my reminiscences of my service life provided a rich source of material for the first book, it seemed to me that my subsequent airline career was relatively repetitive. The fact is that as long as one does one's job properly there is little genuine excitement in a successful airline career, and the same goes for one's parallel family life. How many pages can one fill with "Went to the airport, did the flight planning, flew for seven hours and went to bed"? -- not exactly riveting stuff. And so I discounted any idea of writing of the years from 1968 to 1990, by which time the family had left home to lead successful lives and I was out to grass.

However, it was not many months after retirement that I realized that, whenever I meet up with old colleagues, it is not long before the beer lubricates our tonsils, and we are chuckling away about amusing incidents that happened in London or Frankfurt or wherever else we happened to fly. I wondered if there were enough amusing tales that could be told in polite company to justify a small publication. The only way to find out was to start punching away at the keyboard and see what I could come up with. The result is this little book, which I hope evokes at least a few chuckles from former colleagues, as well as providing some amusement to those whose experience with airlines has been between the sharp and blunt ends, who wish nothing more that a safe journey and to be ready for the trolley lady when she asks,
---**"D'yer want Chicken or Beef?"**

Prologue

Modern aeroplanes are of such incredible technical complexity that there is a myriad of mechanical, electrical and electronic components that can, but rarely do, malfunction in flight. It is for that reason that crews are equipped with comprehensive operating manuals and other reference books, as well as emergency response checklists. No matter how serious, the crew handles the great majority of these occurrences expeditiously and without fuss, and passengers are hardly ever aware that there was a problem in the first place. Even a jet engine failure is hard to notice from a passenger standpoint, except that the captain has an obligation to tell the customers what has occurred and what his actions will be with regard to continuing the flight to destination or land at an intermediate airport. The vast majority of my flights throughout a flying career of forty years were without incident, and in all that time I can remember only two occasions when it was deemed necessary to declare an emergency. Even these ended happily and without harm to man or machine. So you can see that fear of flying is an irrational emotion brought on mainly by ignorance and sensational media reporting.

The selection of aircrew to fly these aeroplanes is rigorous to the extent that only one or two in a thousand initial applicants actually make it all the way to the flight deck of a modern airliner. The survivors of this process are clearly of "the right stuff", possessing to a high degree the aptitude, intelligence, and disciplined mind essential for them to be given the responsibility of taking as many as 600 people into the air in a monster machine weighing up to one million pounds. That does not imply they are paragons of virtue and moral rectitude, far from it. One can find most of the weaknesses that afflict mankind within their ranks, but what is important is that they can bring their strengths to bear when needed. One has only to read some of the many biographies of aviators past to know that they did not suffer fools gladly, but were gifted with enormous sense of humour and wit. I never met a pilot who could not snap to instant response to a situation that demanded his full skill and attention, so please, dear passenger, now that you are suitably reassured, sit back, relax and enjoy my little tales.

A New Life - early days

Some time in 1962 Tommy Atkins and I entered the 99 Squadron crew room, which at that particular time was a mite crowded. "Look at 'em," says Tommy, "they're old men and ought to be put out to grass, not dicing with death flying bleedin' aeroplanes." Whilst I tended to agree with him, for there were indeed a number of senior Flight Lieutenants present, it seemed to me that he was overstating the case. However there *were* one or two present who admitted to having reached the grand old age of forty, so he did have a point. Our own ages at the time were 32 and 31 respectively, and we took our own immortality for granted. Even as we approached the end of our service careers, we certainly did not feel ancient, for after all, our dreaded fortieth birthday was at least 24 months hence, and that is a considerable period when you're young and stupid. Tommy duly departed for the greener pastures of Cyprus Airways, and twelve months later I made my own fond farewells to the Royal Air Force.

My last flight with the Royal Air Force was in late January 1968 and barely seventy-two hours later I was winging my way to Montreal to join my new airline. For a couple of months I would be receiving two incomes, until my RAF service officially expired, but to all intents and purposes I was one of those odd creatures who, for the past twenty-two years, I had treated with a certain amount of disdain, if not contempt. I shouldn't have, I know, for my parents and just about all my relatives and even some friends were **civilians**, with no desire to be anything else.

Whatever feelings of regret that I did have were somewhat mitigated about three weeks later, when I stood resplendent before the tailor in my new Airline uniform. In the mirror I could in fact see a Wing Commander, for I had added a third stripe to the two that I was allowed to wear in the RAF. So anyway, I was after all not quite a civilian, and that was rather comforting.

There were, I think, six of us on my Air Canada conversion course, which lasted about six weeks and was surprisingly comprehensive. I was after all, a fully trained and experienced Transport Command navigator, and knew it all. They were wasting hard cash on training when I could have been productive from the second day. It was about that second day that I realized that perhaps they had a point. There were all sorts of techniques to learn and many bits of equipment with which I was not only unfamiliar, but I had never even heard of. I began to cast a bleak eye back on my Transport Command career, which had ended just a couple of weeks before. This new fangled Loran for instance. I had been flogging all over the world for years using just sunshots and dead-reckoning, and here was this gadget, which we were reliably informed had cost Air Canada just ninety Canadian dollars per set (second hand, of course) that could enable us to accurately fix the aeroplane's position with relative ease, and at timed intervals to avoid straying too far from the beaten track. Then there was a thing called the Sky Compass. This remarkable little device enabled one to determine the exact direction of the sun long after it had disappeared below the horizon. To those who might ask "why bother?" it was rather handy in those areas where the magnetic compass needle was as useful as tits on a bull as it spun in a futile effort to find Magnetic North .

So to cut a long story short, the Air Canada navigation course was indeed a useful few weeks. It took place in the middle of a Montreal winter, which as most Canadians and many British will know, fulfils most of the requirements for arctic survival training, and was a difficult time for us. On our course of six members, only one was a native Canadian. (A few years later I could not have made that statement publicly without implying that Earl Heindrich's ancestry was rooted in wigwams and tomahawks.) Whatever his background, his main value to us was that he was the sole owner of a motor-car, and the only way we could get from our motel to the Air Canada school without incurring the cost of a taxi. Things threatened to become difficult when poor old Earl slipped on the ice and broke an arm. However, the car boasted automatic transmission, and he was able to drive quite well with one arm in a sling. About a week later he slipped again, and this time broke an ankle. This simply delayed each departure by about five minutes as Earl manoeuvred himself in the driver's seat so that his good foot could reach the necessary pedal controls, and his good arm do what was necessary in the gear change and steering department. Much to his credit we did not miss a lecture due to his misfortunes and I really can't remember buying him a single beer in gratitude.

After graduating from the four-week Groundschool, most of us headed for our assigned base - Toronto. There followed a period of flying training, after which we were deemed to be safe to be let loose on our own. The whole course took about six weeks, and thinking back on it now, was probably good value. Particularly important from my point of view was the new system of polar navigation, which was much more efficient than the system in use by RAF Transport Command.

It just remains to remind the reader of the opening paragraph of this chapter. You recall that I was reminiscing on our concept of old age when I was but 31 years of age and my pal Tommy Atkins was a lad of 32. In a large airline it is quite common to turn up for a scheduled flight having never before set eyes upon the rest of the crew. On my first operational flight for my new employer, I arrived in Flight Planning well ahead of the designated crew check-in time and had been working away at the flight plan for half an hour or so, when there was a tap on my shoulder. "Hi, my name's Bert". I looked up. This chap couldn't even remember his own name, for surely this was none other than Methusela! The rather portly old gentleman peered kindly at me through spectacles that seemed to be made from odd bits of glass, and from one ear protruded a large lumpy thing. On closer inspection this turned out to be a hearing aid surmounted by a volume control in the form of a knurled knob. However, he did wear a flat hat, and upon his sleeve were the four gold stripes of authority. Ladies and Gentleman – welcome to the world of Civil Aviation. Where was Tommy Atkins when I needed him?

Characters

After leaving the relative youth of Royal Air Force flying it was sometimes disconcerting to be flying with fellows who were closing on three-score years. We all know that the aging process affects us in different ways, but I think it rather sad when someone we remember as a cheerful forty-year old has become during his sixth decade of life a miserable old sod who looks and acts at least ten years older than his years. This certainly could not be said of Bert Davenport. He looked to me much older than his fifty-seven years, but retained a good sense of humour and was pleasant to fly with, although he tended to rely overmuch on other crew members to keep him up to speed, so to speak. Bert's modus operandi was to let the crew do most of the flight planning and preliminary checks. He then took control and did the take off and initial climb to above 10000 feet, at which point he usually handed the controls to the co-pilot for the next few hours. He would then settle back comfortably in his seat and do as a good captain should and allow his crew to get him safely to London, or wherever the destination happened to be. I do not recall him actually sleeping, but he was certainly in comfortable repose. On one famous occasion this repose was suddenly disturbed by the crew door bursting open and a wide eyed young flight attendant rushing to his seat crying, "Captain, Captain, the galley's on fire!" (One of the galley ovens was overheating and producing a bit of smoke). Bert calmly opened an eye, adjusted his hearing-aid volume and looked up at the young lady with all the benevolence an old gentleman can bestow on an attractive girl, and gently told her to "Call me Bert".

In the days of old there were quite a number of pilots whose personality and sense of humour classified them as "Characters". Sadly there is no room for such gentlemen in today's politically and legally rigid environment, but we certainly had our share of them in "the good old days". I could name quite a number, but will restrict my narrative to just a few.

I once was called before a judge, whose job it was to assess my suitability to join the ranks of Canadian citizenship, and for a time he asked me a few questions on the history and geography of the country. He then inquired as to why, after so many years in Canada, I now wished to be a citizen. I cannot remember my exact reply, but it was to the effect that the original understanding with Air Canada was that the job would last no longer than four or five years, after which I would probably return to Britain. "Oh, you work for Air Canada, do you? Do you happen to know a captain by the name of Bruce Warwick?" I certainly did, and that knowledge ended the formal part of my interview. (In the course of time I was able to replace the tatty piece of paper affirming that I was a "Landed Immigrant"-- always felt like a species of fish with that -- with a bona fide Canadian passport.) The judge spent the next fifteen minutes or so reminiscing about his life in the Royal Canadian Air Force in general and Bruce in particular, who certainly qualified as a "character". Bruce and my judge served together on a ferry squadron flying newly manufactured bombers across "The Pond" to UK. The new planes were desperately needed for the campaign in Europe, and there was little time wasted before sending them on their way to bases in Britain. There were fairly frequent teething troubles with the new aeroplanes, so one had to expect the unexpected, so to speak. On one delivery flight Bruce was the captain and my judge the navigator as they ferried a Boston Bomber across the Atlantic. About halfway across the ocean Bruce handed the controls to the co-pilot and said he was going for a leak. Shortly afterwards the co-pilot exclaimed with alarm that the controls appeared to be seized up and he could not move the ailerons. He told the navigator to find Bruce immediately as it looked like an emergency situation. Bruce was nowhere to be seen in the main cabin and the navigator wondered if he had possibly fallen into space, but all the exits were secure. He then noticed an open hatch leading to the bomb and electrical bays. Here he found our grinning captain sitting on the floor with his arms above his head, firmly grasping the aileron cables. Whether the co-pilot was amused is not recorded, but no doubt a few words were exchanged when the captain regained his rightful seat at the sharp end.

Derek Wells was another captain who had his own individual and slightly eccentric traits. An absolute gentleman both in the air and on layovers, he suffered one minor defect. He could give the appearance of being as blind as a bat. How he passed his routine medicals I do not know, but it was his reading vision that was at fault, so perhaps that was not deemed sufficient to threaten his licence. The navigator of the DC8 sat behind the captain and could see the small area to the left of the captain's seat, which held coffee cup and anything he wished to have at hand, such as newspapers and magazines, or, at a pinch, airport let-down charts. Most pilots consult these charts about half an hour before arrival at the destination airport, and then refer to them at intervals throughout the actual procedures. Poor old Derek was not really capable of this, and once or twice I watched with amusement as, with the aid of a large magnifying glass, he spent whatever time was necessary committing to memory the complete let-down procedure. This would surely have surprised and perhaps alarmed a visitor to the cockpit, who no doubt expected to see a steely-eyed James Bond figure in command.

However, old Derek knew his job as well as any hero of schoolboy comics and he always did a superb job of bringing us all safely back to earth, whatever the weather. The truth was that it was only his short distance vision that had suffered the ravages of age - he could see things at a distance like the proverbial hawk, provided he was wearing his tri-focals, of course. We just hoped and prayed that his short-term memory did not give out at a critical point on the descent to the runway. It must have been the very small print that flummoxed him on the let-down charts, for he could read a paper-back book perfectly well without resorting to a magnifying glass. He often whiled away his time-off period with a good book. He was unable to obtain these books from a lending library, for his novel way (excuse the pun) to keep his place was to tear each page off as he finished it, throwing it in the rubbish bag attached to the trim knob. I once asked him if I could borrow his book after he had finished with it--- can't remember his reply.

A short history of aeroplane drivers

If this was a short history of pilots, I would have to do a lot of homework and delve into the past three thousand years or so, for pilots have been around in one form or another for at least that long, but sadly I am definitely lacking in the fine detail. So this is just an account of the evolution of the aeroplane pilot from the time Orville and his clever brother came up with a contraption that hopped a few hundred feet before hitting the ground, thereby gaining their rightful place in history. That wasn't so long ago, and from then on aviation progressed literally in leaps and bounds to the present day.

For the first few years the new pastime of flying a heavier-than-air machine was the province of wealthy enthusiastic amateurs, but along came the Great War and the opportunity to observe the emplacement of the enemy from above, hopefully to gain tactical advantage by directing one's own cavalry in the right direction. As these new "flying observation posts" were like proverbial sitting ducks and were being shot down in large numbers, a need was created for military "pilots" to take the places of those being given a decent burial.

The only other piece of military equipment that worked in three dimensions was, oddly enough, the horse. So with a strange sort of logic, the generals concluded that the cavalry-whallers could most easily make the transitions from saddle to cockpit. Also the job did not really merit the qualities necessary for commissioned rank, ("after all, it's not much different from riding a motor-cycle, old boy"), but they should not be lower in rank than corporal. So those many airline captains of today who sport four impressive gold stripes are, in fact, the successors of army corporals. In the fullness of time the minimum rank became sergeant, until about the late fifties when commissioned rank was thought most appropriate. The history of civil pilots followed similar logic. For many years the only four-stripers were very senior captains, with their subordinates having to make their way up a steep promotion ladder.

Not too long after that great "conflict to end all conflicts" was over, flying machines improved to the extent that they could be flown quite long distances, and as long as one had a decent map and kept clear of cloud, the pilot could get around without the need for additional crew members. Then someone invented the rudimentary instruments to enable "blind flying". Flying machines got bigger and in the fullness of time passengers were being taken hundreds of miles, often successfully. This gave rise to the necessity for a crew member to work in roughly the same way as ships' navigators, but twenty times faster, and so the flight navigator was born. After that came advances in radio, also requiring a specialist, and so we had the radio officer.

There was one further step in this evolution of flight crews, and that was when designers were able to attach four engines to the aeroplane without the wings falling off in the process. A flight engineer then became necessary. Thus by the end of the second attempt at a war to end all wars, a crew of five (two drivers plus a navigator, radio officer and an engineer) was the norm for four-engine aeroplanes.

However, ego being what it is, and with the advances in electronics, the fellows at the very sharp end began to feel that they could do it all themselves. Also the airline executives were doing their best to increase their profits and tended to reinforce this parsimonious attitude, especially in the United States of America, by reducing the crew complement back to four, then three, crew members. All large airliners still needed full attention paid to the four bloody great engines, so a third member continued to be necessary.

However, the bottom line was still paramount, and things were not helped when a photo was published in an American rag showing a voluptuous air hostess sprawled all over the co-pilot as he sat in his seat wearing, among other things, a lecherous grin. It was a disgruntled flight engineer who had sent that photo to the gleeful rag, so perhaps a plot was set afoot to replace him with a lowly paid junior pilot. In their wisdom the airline owners concluded that "engineers" could in fact be minimally trained and paid lechers, and that is how we ended up in many airlines, with just two, or at the most three, pilots on the flight deck, with no specialists in engines, radios or navigation. Oddly enough, this worked quite well much of the time, but by no means all of the time, and there were numerous incidents, both reported and via the grape-vine, of ginormous (sic) cock-ups of one sort or another. By my estimate, at least a thousand lives have been lost throughout the years due solely to the absence of a specialist navigator.

Be that as it may, when I joined a civilian airline (as a navigator), the flight engineers had been replaced by poorly paid Second Officers with a rudimentary knowledge of engineering and slightly better knowledge of fuel management. This was the situation that existed for many years and only ended when they decided that two pilots were enough, and that is the situation existing today. Anyway, the Second Officer was for some years a fact of life on the large aeroplanes and most of them were splendid fellows, but their real profession was pilot and not engineering. In most cases graduating to the co-pilot's seat was a matter of seniority, which is the reason many of our Second Officers looked at the aging captains with a mixture of morbid curiosity and perverse hope.

And so we come to the real point in this tale, concerning a young Second Officer who was about to be promoted to the "right seat" as we called it. I was the First Officer. The captain was a jovial type who seemed to think that the Second Officer should not surrender his present status without some form of ceremony. I hope you are following me so far.

It seems the captain had had a chat with some of

the Flight Attendants and asked them to think up a suitable departure ceremony. I had no idea what had been planned until two rather attractive Flight Attendants arrived on the flight deck with gleams in their eyes, but otherwise innocent expressions. The next thing I hear is an alarmed yelp from the Second Officer as these two young ladies grabbed him and began an attempt to de-bag him on the spot. He had nowhere to retreat to in the limited space, but he did his best to squeeze himself behind my seat and his own instrument panel. The ladies were not deterred, and continued their task with audible glee and much laughter, and "come on, get 'em off" and "this won't hurt a bit "and "I've got his fly undone" etc. and so forth. I was, of course, fully engrossed in watching this performance and somewhat neglecting my duty to listen out on the radio. I then became aware that in my headphones was a slightly alarmed voice asking what the bloody hell was going on up there, or words to that effect. I couldn't quite figure out who the voice was addressing until I noticed that the victim of this blatant sexual assault was leaning so far back he was pushing on the radio transmit button with his bare bum. The whole episode was being broadcast over an area of hundreds of square miles. We wrested the offending microphone from his buttocks and the girls carried on in radio silence. However, I had to make up a completely implausible story for the Air Traffic Controller, and sadly the girls never fully succeeded, although I did get a fairly good view of a pair of Persil-white Y-fronts.

That young fellow is by now sporting four stripes and perhaps remembers the time when he began the slippery slope up his promotion ladder. Ironically, there is a connection with the opening paragraphs of this chapter, for in his spare time he flew the Hamilton Air Museum's "Richthoven" WW1 triplane, so in a way aviation history had come full circle.

Flat Hats and More Characters

Throughout the ages the wearing of uniforms has been a means of clearly identifying men and women who have a role or occupation whose life depends on being identified by friends and comrades before the shooting starts. The need for uniforms has evolved to the present day, where we have countless organizations that, for various reasons, wish to be clearly visible as belonging to a specific group or organization. As we all know, airlines are no exception, and they dress their aircrew personnel in a distinctive outfit that identifies the employer and hopefully evokes the respect and admiration we all rightfully deserve. This does not always work the way it should. Many years ago a uniformed friend of mine was waiting patiently in his car for his wife to emerge from an exclusive department store in Wales. The wag may question the idea of anything at all in Wales being exclusive, but I will not debate that here. Anyway, a lady emerged from the rotating glass doors of the store, intent on taking a taxi. She saw my friend at the wheel of his vehicle wearing his flat hat, opened the rear door and gave him instructions to take her to the railway station. Without more ado he drove her the two miles to the requested destination, charged her five bob, and was back outside the store just in time to take his wife home.

As airline crew we were expected to be properly dressed when in view of the travelling public, but on the flight deck we could be as informal as we liked. In later years things were relaxed somewhat and one could answer a call of nature wearing just a shirt, tie and a hat (and yes, we *were* required to be fully trousered). So before emerging from the crew compartment one had to go through the rather tedious routine of getting properly attired. It has always been my custom to remove my hat when having a leak – (perhaps a legacy of being brought up in a home with a low-ceilinged outhouse) and upon arrival in the aeroplane toilet I would place my hat alongside the tiny washbasin and get on with the business in hand, so to speak. On one occasion prior to leaving the toilet I pressed the flush button, placed my hat on the toilet seat and was washing my hands when a sudden feeling of dread impelled me to look round at the toilet bowl. (This was many years before I could plead "Senior Moments"). My airline uniform hat was spinning away merrily in the blue flushing fluid. Luckily I retrieved it before it was sucked into the plumbing system, and with due respect to company policy, shook the dripping chapeau a few times, placed it gently upon my head and very hurriedly returned to my crew station. I cannot remember whether I subsequently applied for a new cap, and if I did, what reason I would have given, but my warped sense of humour would have perhaps amused the storeman. Needless to say, my motto from then on was "Look before you leak!"

For those occasions when the call of nature was likely to be prolonged, it was nice to have a bit of reading material, (I'm told "it's a Man thing") which I usually managed to sneak in without it being noticed by a flight attendant or customer. This was not always successful and a flight attendant once remarked with a sly smirk as I opened the toilet door, "Number Two?"

While we are on the subject of flat hats, I recall with great amusement the time when Harry Campton and I were operating a charter aeroplane to some destination where no doubt the customers were pursuing what was implied in the advert: "sea, sun and sex", not necessarily in that order. In those days of rather complicated and often restrictive government regulations as to what, when and where the would-be travelling public could be taken, there arose a market niche dealing in charter flights. As I recall it, a travel agent, or even an individual, could approach an airline and for an agreed price could charter an aeroplane and crew to fly to and from a particular holiday destination. He then flogged the seats to the general public, promising at least two out of the three above-mentioned attractions. The final ticket price per passenger was, of course, mainly influenced by the cost of the charter and the profit the operator wished to make. The practice is not so prevalent these days but in the '60s and '70s there were a number of airlines specializing in this type of flying, and the major airlines participated when they could spare aeroplanes from scheduled routes.

It is sufficient to add that charter flying tapped a market of unsophisticated and inexperienced passengers of modest means, who were out for as good a time as could be obtained for the few hundred bucks they had paid. It was quite common for many of the passengers to assume that the holiday began on arrival at the departure airport, where they sought out the bar and slurped away until departure time. By the time they embarked many of them would be slightly under the influence, some were at the obnoxious stage and one or two paralytically sloshed. These latter posed no problem. It was the second category where the hazards lay and it was for this reason that these flights were not too popular among the cabin staff. I am sure that there are many former flight attendants of that period who could relate horror stories of these flights. Thankfully the operating crew was, in the main, insulated from these shenanigans and only ventured out of the flight deck for the occasional pee. Now and again a captain was called upon to exert his authority and perhaps his muscles to quell a nasty incident, but thankfully things rarely got that bad.

So now I have set the stage for the flight mentioned in the first sentence of this rather tedious account. I think the flight was to Barbados or Antigua, but it was certainly somewhere in the Caribbean. As has been implied, many of the passengers were well oiled when they boarded and it seemed they belonged to an organized group and knew each other. They were cavorting hither and thither throughout the aeroplane, singing and shouting and having a generally uproarious time. While all this was going on, we on the flight deck were going about our duties in our usual conscientious manner, with yours truly busy keeping the aircraft as close as possible to the planned course. Our solitude was suddenly disturbed in the form of a partly attired young woman bursting onto the flight deck. She was clad in just a dainty pair of panties and a bra, and we extended to her the courtesy of our immediate and undivided attention for the few moments she was with us. She said she wouldn't stay long, but could she please have the captain's hat. Taking into account the position of the captain's seat and that I was in his line of desired vision, poor old Harry could only get a partial glimpse of this delectable and exuberant creature. Whether he gave his permission or not, she was handed the hat from the crew closet and a second later all was peace once more, with just four bemused aircrew wondering if it was a dream.

After a minute or so, the purser returned to the cockpit to give us a blow-by-blow report, so to speak. The young lady was now completely starkers, and was dancing up and down the aisle using Harry's hat as her one and only prop. What on earth she was doing with it is anyone's guess who was not there, but by the sounds of hilarity emanating throughout the passenger cabin she was getting unanimous and enthusiastic encouragement. The performance went on for ten minutes or so, after which she probably ran out of ideas – well, how much can you do with a pilot's cap? In due course the amateur stripper replaced her clothing and returned the cap with thanks. Poor old Harry studied it wistfully for a few moments and muttered something about not being properly compensated (I shall not relate his exact words) and continued with his duties.

When I began this narrative never did I think I could say much about flat 'ats, but I seem to have done myself proud. There is just one further anecdote concerning hats lurking in my addled brain before I leave the subject forever.

In 1964 Trans Canada Airlines was renamed Air Canada. This is significant to this little tale as it is the year that all the pilots on the airline obtained the newly designed Air Canada cap. Assuming that a cap would last on average four years, in 1983 most of those pilots were on their fifth hat – except Warren Danforth, who still carried, and very occasionally wore, the hat obtained from Company stores in 1964. Warren is a tall and rather distinguished looking Englishman with an Oxford accent and in many ways your stereotypical airline pilot – he is also a "character" in the way previously described. As with many distinguished English gentlemen of good pedigree he did not seem to have much interest in his appearance, and the necessity to have a cap somewhere about his person – rarely on his head – was a bothersome nuisance. Over the years the hat in question had not so much worn, as decomposed, and the supervisory pilots did their best to no avail to get Warren to obtain a new one. Maybe it had become a bit of a fetish with him, I do not know. Then came the time that he elected to fly the Queen of the Fleet, the Boeing 747. He successfully completed the course without a problem and all that was necessary was to have his licence endorsed for the new machine. Finally, the 747 Chief Pilot saw his chance. "Warren, I am not signing this licence until you get a new cap." And so Warren Danforth was compelled to pay a visit to Stores and obtained the new chapeau – and this is the hat he was wearing for his last flight in 1990, so he got a good fourteen years service from it, and I like to think it was accorded a place of honour in his compost bin. I flew with Warren on and off over the years and we got on well together. I always had a quiet chuckle at his insouciant attitude towards his appearance. Maybe it had something to do with the fact that on his days off he looked after a flock of sheep. I never saw him in that role, but it is easy to imagine him with a shepherd's crook and his trousers held up with binder twine. I would quickly add that he would have been the most distinguished looking shepherd in Canada. The last time I flew with him was in 1989 and, as we were donning our jackets and attempting to look dapper before we emerged from the flight deck, I happened to notice that his pilots' wings were an old design that had been replaced in 1970. "You must be very fond of those pilots' wings, Warren" I remarked. He looked down somewhat bewildered and replied, "Well not really, Windy, they came with the jacket".

Concessionary Travel

One of the frustrations that airline employees often have to suffer is that upon their return from a holiday that involved a flight, envious neighbours comment, "Oh, you got there for nothing". Well, many years ago that may have been true, but for the past 25 or so years concessionary travel for airline employees has been anything but free, and what with having to cough up the full whack of taxes, I am sure that my annual travel costs are not much less than the average Joe or Jo-ess. In any case, I have bitter memories of being treated like a refugee from Outer Mongolia when attempting to get a "free" space available seat on one of my employer's aeroplanes; waiting hours, and sometimes days to complete the planned journey. In spite of all this, I must admit that airline concessionary travel has been a great benefit over the years and I should certainly not complain. However, I know that many airline employees dislike the hassle of so-called "free" travel and prefer to buy confirmed seats. At the time I am writing this I have just returned from Australia, where I was able to purchase confirmed seats at just about the same price as if I were using airline concession fares, so those envious neighbours can themselves travel quite cheaply if they do their homework. Another disadvantage of "free" travel is that one is often subject to different rules and protocols when travelling on an airline pass. Things are much better now, but at one time it seemed to me that at every airport, airline staff had devised ways of humiliating employees seeking space available seats. The moment a passenger agent identified one as a "con" (short for concessionary passenger) the rules of politeness and common courtesy often went out the window. A fairly common response was words to the effect: "Not much chance, but go over there and wait with those other poor slobs." You knew exactly where to go because in the sea of denim, tee shirts and grotty sandals would be a small group of prospective passengers dressed like Jehovah's

Witnesses on the prowl, with the fellows in jackets, ties and nicely creased trousers and their ladies in posh frocks. The only times in their little lives that the small sons of employees were compelled to don a tie were weddings, funerals and when presenting themselves at the check-in desk. That was the rule - dress posh or you don't get aboard. I once had the humiliating experience of having my grandson rejected for travel because he was wearing jeans. Ninety-nine point nine percent of small boys cover their dirty little legs with denim, and there was I, made to feel like Dickens' Mr. Bumble. We had to plough through his luggage to find something acceptable, and as he had packed his bag himself (and I use the word "packed" advisedly), it wasn't easy.

Things are much more relaxed now, but denim is still banned, a rule that I tend to agree with. Historians will surely label the present years as the "the age of scruff". At London's Heathrow, if we *were* lucky and had a boarding pass thrust into our sticky hands, we then had about half an hour to check in our baggage, go through border control, rush into duty-free for a bottle and two hundred (the customs limit for liquor and fags (sic) and then run about five hundred yards to the departure gate. (London Airports seem to have an unwritten rule that moving walkways will always be unserviceable in the direction one wishes to hurry!) Other departure cities had different procedures, but in nearly every one they managed to pack in at least half an hour of unnecessary stress when dealing with employees with "free" passes. So my point is that pass travel is not all that it is cracked up to be, but nevertheless I have persisted over the years and been rewarded with seeing places that I would never have otherwise visited. So, scattered throughout these pages are just a few recollections from the dim and distant past, as Audrey and I and the kids took advantage of employee discounted travel.

"Oh, Island in the Sun"

Our first attempt to use an employee pass was a total failure. Having got the kids all psyched up for a few days in Vancouver, we were turned down flat at the check-in desk. The passenger agent rather smugly informed us that all flights that day were overbooked and we wouldn't have an "earthly". We must have given the children the impression that the trip was a sure thing, for when I told them we were returning home, the two older boys became somewhat rebellious, and the youngest burst into tears. My standing as head of the household went down from a about a "nine" to something in the minus column.

The allocation of space available seats to employees was based strictly according to company seniority, to the extent that the day one joined could be critical in tight situations. So it required the passage of time to improve one's chances of getting where one wished to go on the date one wished to travel.

About a year after the failed attempt to fly to Vancouver, I decided to try our luck again, and we made plans to visit Barbados during the children's school Spring break. In the course of my work I had been to Barbados a number of times and it seemed to me that it would be a welcome escape from the miseries of the Canadian winter. I had negotiated a one week rental of a two-bedroom flat. In a bid for redemption after the last fiasco, I had assured the children that our chances were much better this time and they pumped up their enthusiasm to fever pitch. I would be in *real* trouble if we failed again. To get into the spirit of the occasion they wore airline-style caps and carried small suitcases that resembled little flight-bags.

Much to my relief we were given boarding passes at the check-in desk and all was sweetness and light in the family department. Audrey looked very nice in her summer frock, I was as dapper as polyester and nylon would allow, and the children looked neat and tidy as we headed for the boarding gate.

Once airborne and the seat-belt signs were *distinguished* (quite a common malapropism among our Gallic flight attendants) - "in preparation for our landing please *distinguish* your cigarettes"- I did not smoke, but was tempted to ask all puffing passengers to raise their glowing fags towards the ceiling. Anyway, the captain duly switched off the seat belt sign, and this was the signal for David and Chris to head rearwards for the toilets. No doubt they were answering a call of nature, but they used the opportunity to plunder the toilets of small tablets of soap, sundry toiletries and any other item provided by the management for the comfort of the customers. In our defence, Audrey and I did not discover these Fagin-like tendencies until we were comfortably established in the rented flat and the contents of the kids' little flight bags were revealed. A warning was issued at that point and presumably they left a reasonable amount of soap in the washrooms on subsequent flights. Anyway, we had enough soap to last us about three months after that particular holiday.

The rented flat turned out to be located on the first floor of a two-storey building, with a similar flat below. We had indeed been lucky with my choice of accommodation. The building was on the edge of a magnificent sand beach, with shops and some restaurants just a short walk away. We arrived at the flat early in the afternoon and were unpacking and generally preparing to start to enjoy the holiday as soon as possible, when a large shadow appeared at the patio door. Standing there was a tall and rather portly gentleman wearing bathing shorts and a flamboyant Hawaiian shirt. "Hello, my name is Bruce, welcome to Barbados". (This was my first meeting with Captain Bruce Warwick, who has already loomed large in these memoirs.) Introductions were made all-round and he invited us to come down to his quarters to enjoy a sundowner at any time, day or night - it certainly did not have to be sundown.

We took advantage of his kind offer that evening,

after which I decided that his unstinting hospitality was definitely a hazard to my health. He had already been in occupation for about a week and during that time had succeeded in converting his living room into a well-stocked pub. It was certainly out of bounds to the kids, notwithstanding Bruce's invitation to come any time they needed a "small lemonade".

In fact we did not see very much of Bruce after that. I think that we were probably a bit of a disappointment to him on the imbibing front, but in any case, he spent quite a lot of time away from his quarters. Where he went I do not know, but within a short distance was the locally notorious Harry's Bar, in which, among other questionable activities, one could be invited to join in the party game entitled "find de hole" involving young ladies of questionable calling. They have since somewhat dignified the name, but not the rules, by calling it "Lap Dancing". Anyway, it is but conjecture, but Bruce could easily have been spending some of his time there, although he was too much of a gentleman to indulge in party games. One morning after breakfast we were walking along the beach for a swim and met Bruce returning to his flat, clad in a flamboyant shirt and what seemed to be swimming shorts. I greeted him with a cheery "Good morning, Bruce, been for an early morning swim?" "No" he replied, "just on my way to bed". Such stamina was to be admired and he never changed. He was always cheerful, good natured and the perfect gentleman, but a hard act to follow on the social front. Years later, a colleague met him on his houseboat in Florida. It was some years after his retirement and very sadly he was suffering from an incurable cancer. His comment then was a cheerfully philosophical "I'll shortly be setting out upon the greatest adventure of all". That was Bruce, and I like to think that he is enjoying that adventure, but he can be assured that he left behind many amusing memories in this world.

Deadheading is not always dull

Before I left the Royal Air Force, I had given hardly a thought to the way civilian aircrews achieve the task in hand – namely to ensure that passengers are transferred efficiently and safely from one airport to another in accordance with both their wishes and the fellows running the airline. In the Royal Air Force it was fairly straightforward. One was tasked to fly an aeroplane to say, Cyprus, have a nap, and the following day fly the same aeroplane back to Lyneham, or wait to pick up another 'plane that would be "slipping" through that location. We had a limited fleet and a limited number of destinations, so tasking aircrews was not a complex problem, although there were some famous cock-ups throughout the years.

Now, imagine an airline with a hundred aeroplanes and as many destinations and attempt to work out a schedule that conforms with a published time-table, a set of fairly rigid working rules for the aircrew, utilization of the aeroplanes so that they are mostly in the air earning their interest payments and umpteen other costs. Not easy. I shall not dwell much further on this, except to mention that in order to achieve efficiency and keep aircrew to a minimum, it is often necessary to "deadhead" crews from one place to another so that they can be put to work as soon as possible after they have had the statutory rest period.

Although we had a definite time limit with regard to maximum time on flying duty, no limit was in effect for subsequent deadheading. One could land at 7am, by which time you were close to the fourteen-hour crew-duty limit. However, crew members often then had to check in for the passenger flight to the final destination specified on the crew tasking sheet. One could wait up to three hours before the deadheading flight departed, plus a couple of hours for the flight itself, and at least an hour by taxi to the designated layover hotel. A further frustration was often to be told that the room wasn't prepared. So you can see that a flight from say, Toronto to Zurich with a subsequent deadhead to Vienna and finally hitting the sack at about 2pm, could entail a total time of up to 20 hours. Add to that the fact that the original take-off was the on the previous evening; that one had in any case been up most of that day, and one can easily appreciate that our crew member was an extremely tired lad when he did finally enter his assigned hotel room.

Still, the money was good, so we got very little sympathy or understanding from the public or those who chose to comment on their behalf.

One can reasonably conclude that the necessity to deadhead after an overnight flight across "The Pond" was a decidedly tedious business, but being the relatively vigorous and imaginative ex-Air Force chaps that we were, we found much to keep us amused and relieve the boredom.

I well remember one occasion when I had the pleasure of flying with Second-Officer Albert Alworth and First-Officer Roy Sterling, admirably led by Captain Rob Unslow. Our flight from Toronto was to Frankfurt, after which we had about two hours to kill before boarding our deadhead flight to Vienna. We spent some of the time in the airport workers' canteen on the lower level of the terminal building. It was about 7.30 am and there were not many customers about. At the next table sat an American airman accompanied by a rather buxom and attractive Fraulein, who appeared to be there to see him off the premises after perhaps a night of dissolute pleasure in a nearby hostelry. That last bit is purely conjecture on my part, but there was not much visual doubt that the relationship was a lot more than platonic and that this was a fond farewell of some sort. The lady was certainly attractive enough to divert Roy's and my attention away from the drowsy mumblings between us. Unfortunately for them, Albert and Rob were facing away from the table in question. The lady began to work on an apparent itch in the vicinity of her ample bosom. This quickly got the full attention of Roy and a few microseconds later I followed his gaze in the direction of the offending itch. Obviously the lady's fingernails were failing to find relief, and almost absentmindedly she lowered the zip of her blouse, reached inside and much to the pleasure of Roy and myself, extracted her handsome right breast. She was then clearly able to relieve her itch (but not ours!). Roy could contain himself no longer. "She's got it out!" he exclaimed. By the time that Rob and Albert had figured out which lady had got what out, the breast was back in its size D garment of repose and the zip being closed. I thought I detected a mischievous glint from the lady's eye, but that could have been my imagination. It certainly added a touch of spice to an otherwise tedious early morning deadhead to the city of Johann Strauss!

Whilst my memories pleasurably linger in Germany and Austria, I recall an occasion when I was required to position myself in Munich after working an overnight flight to Frankfurt. All the above issues applied. It was morning; I was very tired and had to wait a considerable time before boarding the Lufthansa flight to Munich. My mood was not improved when I discovered that my assigned seat was next to a nun in full habit, and I was about to come under ecclesiastical scrutiny. To add insult to idolatry, beneath her wimple she possessed a very attractive face and I could perhaps be forgiven (after due penance, of course) for my mind wandering in the direction of Julie Andrews in her role as Maria. Anyway, I kept my tie on, sat up straight, and took on a demeanor of respect and rectitude. In due course the drinks trolley arrived and I requested a coffee with cream and sugar. You could have knocked me down with a Kookaburra feather when in a strong Australian accent my sister companion asked – "ave yer got any beer?" My rectitude promptly disappeared into the surrounding billowing clouds, as for the first and only time in my life, I began to chat about worldly affairs with a real live nun. It turned out that she was on her way home for a spot of leave from some seminary or other in the Land of OZ, and was looking forward enormously to meeting relatives and friends after many years away from her home in Dachau (my questions on that score remain unanswered) – obviously enough years to gain a strong Australian accent and develop a taste for "Fosters". Upon arrival in Munich she was met by an enthusiastic party of friends and relations who were obviously delighted to see her again, – and I was reminded that the tale of Maria was by no means unique.

One of my favourite deadhead memories is of a flight to Shannon, Ireland, where, for a change, I was given a hotel *before* proceeding to my next port of call, which was Frankfurt. The onward flight would be by PanAm early the following morning and I would pick up the ticket from the local staff. After a relaxing evening and a reasonable night's sleep I was out of bed at the appointed hour, and half an hour later was outside the hotel awaiting my taxi. No taxi in sight, and after about fifteen minutes I began to get concerned. Remember, we are in Southern Ireland and things there seem to go along at a very leisurely pace.

It took some time to contact someone in authority as to the whereabouts of my transport, which in any case had to come from Limerick – about ten miles away. Eventually a taxi skidded into the hotel forecourt and a very apologetic driver got me to the airport thirty minutes late. Upon arrival at Shannon I could see the PanAm aeroplane on the tarmac and clearly there would be very little time for me to collect my ticket and go through the usual departure formalities. There was only one snag – but a rather large one – the Air Canada Office was closed with no personnel to be seen. I asked at the PanAm check-in counter if they had my ticket, but to no avail. I returned to the office and banged on the door in the hope that perhaps there was a sleeping Irishman on the other side. No response. Now panic was beginning to set in. By this time my flight was due to leave within a very few minutes and there seemed no hope I could be aboard by the time it did. Finally our agent – an amiable chap named Patrick – arrived, unlocked the door to the office and assured me that "everything's foin sorr – your ticket is in the safe and we'll have you on board in a jiffy, Sorr, -- now where did I put the key to the safe?" "Begorrah", (forgive me for taking liberties with the vernacular) "I tink that Brendan (his colleague) has taken the bloddy thing home with him." No ticket, no Brendan and it seemed no hope. Patrick made a mad dash around the office hoping the key was lying around somewhere. Finally he shrugged his Celtic shoulders and said to me "come with me sorr, we'll see if we can get you on board anyway".

I followed him through the maze of offices and passages of Shannon Airport, and we shortly emerged on to the tarmac where my PanAm aeroplane was showing signs of imminent departure. The aeroplane entry door was closed and the passenger steps were about to be removed. Without hesitation Patrick was up the steps and banging on the door, which was shortly reopened by a curious attendant clad in a life jacket as she prepared to tell the passengers what to do if they were dunked in the Irish Sea.

There followed a hurried discussion and thirty seconds later Patrick shouted down to me "It's okay, Sorr, I've fixed it and you don't need the ticket. We'll sort it out later when Brendan arrives." Not only that, but they sat me in first class and I enjoyed a gourmet, but thoroughly illegal, breakfast as I winged my way towards Frankfurt. Of course, that was long before fanatics and lunatics created the need for much more rigorous security procedures.

Life in the stratosphere
Strangers in the Night

During the winter months Air Canada concentrated much of its attention to fulfilling the demand for Canadians to escape winter for a few days (or weeks), and there were daily flights to the main Florida destinations, as well as the Inner and Outer Caribbean. In late '60s early '70s I flew many trips to Antigua and Barbados, and very nice they were too, with the planned night-stop in a holiday hotel by the beach, and the prospect of a rum punch or two to assist peaceful slumber before the following day's return to reality. Many of the customers were flying on some sort of package deal and in many respects the flights were similar to the charters I have already described, with many of the passengers in holiday mood from the time they checked in. The main difference between these flights and charters was that the aeroplane was configured to accommodate different classes of passenger, and notwithstanding the extra cost there was a respectable demand for first class, much to the satisfaction of the head office. The difference between first class passengers on the flights across "The Pond" and those going to southern climes was that the majority of the former did not pay their own fare – it was paid by the company they worked for, which no doubt passed the cost down the line to you and me in one form or another. . Hence the development into what is now called "Business Class". Those going south were usually the genuinely "idle rich", who were prepared to fork out the ticket money from their own resources.

And so it came to pass that a presumably idle rich fellow and his female companion boarded the 5pm flight to Barbados, were duly seated in comfort in First Class. The flight attendant was at the ready with a nice smile, toilet kits containing a tiny toothbrush, an even tinier tube of toothpaste and a pair of socks without heels. They were then handed two glasses of champagne, which they both knocked back in the style that rich people are wont to do. It was about this point where their behaviour tended to deviate from that of the truly wealthy. They commenced a bit of quiet snoggery, the nature of which caused the flight attendant to look discreetly in another direction. Shortly after take-off they began to receive the first class service they had paid for, including pre-dinner drinkies and a five-course meal, washed down with copious quantities of excellent wine. What with their napkins, the dinner trays and all the fine china, their amorous movements were somewhat curtailed, but by the time the fruit and nuts arrived they were striving once more to explore each other's most intimate parts. How did we at the sharp end know all this? We were getting a blow-by-blow (excuse the pun) account from the flight attendant, who was frankly getting increasingly alarmed at the whole business. Once the trays were taken away our couple moved to the small first class lounge at the front of the cabin and, according to our cabin staff commentator, things were reaching the critical stage that in some species requires the use of a bucket of cold water. It looked very much as if copulation was about to take place across the lounge table and in full view of the staff. By this time the door to the crew compartment was opening and closing with such rapidity that it was creating a draft. I think the implication was that the captain should take a hand, but this he was loath to do, and continued to sit firmly strapped in with no intention of going anywhere else, least of all to ask a couple of middle-aged copulaters to cease and desist. Suddenly, and without warning, the lady's ardour and demeanour began to cool rapidly – no idea why - and she began using language more appropriate to some of the folk enjoying the less opulent delights of Hospitality Class. We continued to get regular reports, because now it seemed that the lady was threatening physical violence. Apparently the gentleman in the proceedings was completely nonplussed and wished to discontinue the encounter as quickly as possible. She then cranked up her language a notch and started belting him about the body and face, at which point he managed with difficulty to extricate himself and return to his seat. In the circumstances one would have expected her to follow him, but in fact she stayed where she was, for the simple reason that she was blind drunk and quite incapable of moving without assistance. By this time there was perhaps an hour to go before landing and our last report was that she was noisily sleeping it off. Meanwhile, her unfortunate companion, who had not been violent, began to explain to the flight attendant the circumstances of the relationship. It was barely twenty-four hours old and its genesis had been in a downtown bar in Toronto. He had made this lady's acquaintance and things had progressed to the stage where he suggested they pop off at his expense to Barbados for a couple of nights of sun, sea and the other thing. He now wanted nothing whatsoever to do with her and hoped to never set eyes upon her again. After landing he shot off down the steps like a little bunny, leaving the woman still snoring in the first class lounge. It took a long time to wake her up, but even then she was still completely inebriated and totally incapable of self-perambulation. She was then (correctly) classed as disabled, and after ten minutes or so a wheelchair arrived at the bottom of the passenger steps. It took two strong ground staff personnel to manipulate her down the steps and into the wheelchair. My last sight of her was when she had been pushed about halfway to the terminal building, at which point the wheelchair with its occupant had fallen on its side and she was lying on the tarmac accompanied by a perplexed ground agent. The moral of this story is obvious, but I have no doubt that countless similar incidents have occurred since that warm night in Barbados many years ago.

Bathing Interlude

In 1961 Air Canada acquired a small fleet of Vickers Vanguards to be utilised on medium and short haul flights within Canada. They were to be crewed by just a pilot and a co-pilot with a jump seat in the cockpit for route-checkers or additional personnel when required. A year or two later, a bright spark in the planning department decided that these aeroplanes had the range to operate to Bermuda and the Outer Caribbean. There was one small snag. In order to satisfy Ministry of Transport requirements, a third crew member would be required in the shape of a licenced navigator. A further requirement was that the navigator must have sufficient equipment to calculate the aircraft position, and a flat surface of some sort on which to work his magic. Accordingly, a small navigator station was squeezed into the narrow space behind the co-pilot, and a Loran set installed in the passageway connecting the passenger cabin with the chaps at the sharp end. All this was achieved to the satisfaction of the powers that be, and in the fullness of time a reasonable profit was being made from this route.

I am given to understand that Airline Management did not regard the Vanguard as a particularly good aircraft, as its maintenance costs were higher than expected, but from the crew point of view it was a nice machine, relatively easy to fly and a comfortable and roomy flight deck. That was before they started squeezing in extra bits of electronic equipment – and navigators. However, we usually got along splendidly, and efficiently delivered the customers to their desired destination of either Bermuda or further down the line to Antigua and Barbados. The main reason they were travelling there was to escape for a week or two from the Canadian winter. In other words it was warm, which meant that during the hour or so the aeroplane was on the ground to refuel and pick up passengers, the crew compartment, with its generously sized windows, went from a reasonable 75deg Fahrenheit just after landing to something evocative of the Sahara Desert at mid-day. Yes, I *am* reminded that we probably had air-conditioning, but it did not always reach us at the sharp end. To add insult to injury, at Bermuda we were parked about a hundred yards from, and well within sight of, a beautiful beach with its turquoise water and the occasional nubile maiden cavorting in the surf.

One could only look longingly at this sight and hope that perhaps at some time in the future we could garner the money and the time to emulate our lucky passengers, and spend a few days in this paradise.

There was an occasion when our dear old captain, looking seemingly helplessly upon this scene, could stand it no longer. "I'm going for swim, who's coming with me?" "But we've only got 45 minutes to take-off," was the reply of the junior co-pilot. "Don't bloody care, I'm going anyway, come on Nav, get your swimming trunks, we'll leave the bleedin' co-pilot to look after the shop". "No you bloody won't. If you go, I go," responded the rebellious First Officer. And so we rummaged into our overnight cases and fished out the necessary garments. In my case my natty brief swimming shorts and, for a makeshift towel, yesterday's uniform shirt from my laundry bag, then departed via the front door of the aeroplane for the nearby beach. Quickly disrobing and donning our swimwear we then spent a glorious twenty minutes or so enjoying the warm Bermudan waters.

The twenty minutes was up almost before we knew it, and in fact had become almost thirty. The scheduled departure was just fifteen minutes away and there we were, still in our swim suits, soaking wet, feet covered in sand, and in the near distance a line of passengers making their way up the steps and into the interior of the pilotless and navigatorless craft.

As quickly as we could we wiped ourselves down with our makeshift towels, donned our uniforms and made our way back to the aeroplane. By this time the forward entrance door had been closed and we were compelled to enter via the rear door, squeezing past those passengers still standing in the aisle. We certainly received some odd looks as we progressed down the cabin, but put on a demeanour that we hoped suggested that nipping out for a mid-day plunge in the ocean was quite a normal occurrence.

I do not remember if we actually managed to depart on time, but we were certainly refreshed and feeling better for the experience. About four hours later we were on our way home, tackling the snow- covered roads and sub zero temperatures, with a dip in a warm ocean on a hot day just a distant memory – or was it a dream?

A Wing and a Prayer

It was a quiet and starry night as we headed towards London on the nightly scheduled flight. The starry bit was important to me in order that I might periodically use the sextant to fix the aircraft's position with uncanny accuracy. In those days Doppler navigation was in its adolescence, if not its infancy, and the idea of satellite navigation was right out of science fiction. I was working hard and diligently on these navigational requirements, when suddenly the purser appeared on the flight deck with a request. "There is a fellow in first class who wants to know which way is East." Well of course, that mildly provoked my curiosity, and I poked my head through the flight deck door. To my amusement I saw this chap dressed in a posh frock, with a white cap upon his head and a book in his hand, pacing up and down the aisle, at the same time muttering some mumbo-jumbo or other.

Well, we all know, of course, that God is Church of England, so this seemed to be some sort of heathen ritual. Now before the reader picks me up on a point of accuracy, I am perfectly aware that C of E clergy address their flock on a Sunday wearing a posh frock. This was not Sunday and we were not in a church. It was also long before our home and native land opened wide its doors to people other than those whose ethnic origin was mostly European, so I was a bit hazy about the beliefs of our coloured brethren. Someone suggested that he was probably a Mohammedan (what we call in these modern times, a Muslim). He could have been that or any one of a number of the unenlightened to whom the direction of East is important. It was of course important to me, because that was roughly the direction of London and a pint of Watneys Best Bitter. I then said to the purser that if our putative praying passenger was of the Islamic persuasion, he probably wanted not East, but the direction of Mecca. His normal habitat was probably in North Africa or Arabia, and East may certainly have been appropriate, but here at latitude 55 degrees North and around 30 degrees West, his desired point of reverence was much more likely to be in the South East quadrant, and I did my best to oblige. I instructed the purser to tell him to stand looking forward and then turn about 20 degrees to the right, where he should be in the required direction within a degree or two. The purser gave him my advice, at which point the worshipper placed on the cabin floor a small mat upon which he knelt and supplicated in the direction indicated by the good old navigator. Perhaps in the fullness of time, our passenger of long ago sits in paradise wondering what in heaven to do with the sixty virgins he was given as a reward for knowing the exact direction of Mecca -- just a thought.

Spring Break - Alpine style

My first full winter in Canada was that of 1968/69 during which I spent my time, when not at work, in a state of semi-hibernation indoors. Until then I had not paid much attention to the term "Cabin Fever", associating it more with life in the tundra than an urban district just outside the metropolis of Toronto. But believe me, unless one is skilled in a winter sport, there are not too many options for outdoor activity without risking life and limb in subfreezing temperatures and icy surfaces.

I therefore resolved that at the onset of the following winter I would learn to ski. In December of that year I saw an advertisement in the local paper inviting people to sign up for skiing lessons with the Georgetown YMCA, and promptly applied. Somewhat to my surprise, but not necessarily my delight, it turned out to be an all-ladies class (plus me), but I was made to feel welcome and within a few weeks I had learnt the fundamentals of staying upright on a pair of narrow planks. I did at least purchase the skis from a proper sports shop. A mate of mine, who wished to save a bit of cash, bought a couple of pine boards from a hardware store and nailed a pair of boots to them. Needless to say, he didn't learn a great deal about the art of skiing, and spent much of the time on his bum.

Audrey did not share my enthusiasm for the sport, but like the good soul she was she accompanied me to the local slopes at weekends and made a few tentative moves in a downward direction. The boys had quickly learned to ice skate and had no trouble at all learning the rudiments of skiing.

And it came to pass that for the school Spring break of 1972, Audrey and I agreed to spend it in the Austrian Alps. From the short and shallow slopes in Ontario to the Austrian Alps can truly be described as a bold move - some would use the word foolhardy or bonkers or what you will. Anyway, if nothing else, we could enjoy the food and the scenery and it seemed a good idea at the time and this many years later I have not changed my opinion.

Somewhat to my relief we were successful in our first attempt at getting seats on the evening flight to Zurich, from where we took a train to Zel am Zee and thence by bus to our destination, Kaprun – a total travel time of about twenty hours, so we were a little "whacked" by the time we arrived.

One could not have chosen a more scenic setting, and our hotel was comfortable, provided good meals and a friendly atmosphere. I have fond memories of Willy, a vacationing German naval officer, who most mornings "reported" at our breakfast table, stood to attention, clicked his heels and with a little bow wished us "Guten Morgen". I think he had taken a shine to meine Fraulein, but that is mere conjecture. Anyway, for me the war was over, and I couldn't wait get our own family parade together and march smartly to join the queue at the cable car station for the journey to the slopes.

It was necessary to start as early as 6am, which would get us to the slopes by about 7.30, in time to join our assigned ski classes at 8am. You may ask what need we had for lessons having "done the course" back home, but there is a world of difference between lessons in Ontario and those given by experienced Alpine ski instructors. In true Teutonic fashion, punctuality was paramount and any tardiness meant hunting about 50 acres of snow for one's ski class. We had been assigned classes according to the assessment of the chief ski instructor. Michael and Christopher were together, but the rest of us were scattered among various groups of budding Jean Claude Killys. It did not help Audrey's lack of enthusiasm for the sport to find that apparently none of her classmates could speak English. The lessons finished at mid-day, after which we were expected to consolidate our new skills on our own until about 3.30pm, at which time we joined the queue for the return journey to the hotel.

All this physical activity meant that by the evening we were all pretty nigh tuckered out and it was a great pleasure to relax in the "Aktung Stoof", the very pleasant pub attached to our hotel, which served a multitude of healing waters. It was our rendezvous of choice, and we often arranged to meet at such and such a time in the "Aktung Stoof". " I'm going upstairs for a bath and will meet you in the "Aktung Stoof" at about six o clock", would be a typical remark. The reason we knew the name of the bar was that it was painted on a signboard at the top of the short flight of steps. Towards the end of our holiday it suddenly dawned on me that the "Achtung Stoeff" as we called it (I deliberately misspelt it to put the clever clogs reader off the scent) was simply the warning in German to "Mind the Step". So all week we had been agreeing to meet each other in the "Mind the Step"!

The skiing itself went surprisingly well and even Audrey enjoyed most of the holiday, although I did once come across her sitting on her bum apparently unable to regain a vertical position, with a tear or two on her cheek and the telling remark "and you call this fun?" The official end of the ski course was on the Friday and was celebrated by a course get-together in the bar of one of the many hotels.

Because it seemed that Audrey would be very lonely among her unilingual German classmates, I decided to join her party rather than my own. Much to her (and my) disgust it turned out that most of her class could in fact speak passable English. Audrey was more than a little miffed, but all was forgiven about fifteen minutes after she had sampled her first stein of Jaeger Tea. This is a deceptively pleasant-tasting infusion of rum, spices and tea, possibly invented as an attempt to revive the dead. To the unsuspecting it could easily do the opposite. About two hours later we managed by sheer determination and mutual spousal support in the strictly physical sense, to find our way home.

The following day was the final day of the holiday

and, as the ski lessons were over, we were more or less a united family as we commenced our day's skiing on the mountain. After about an hour the boys wished to be a bit more adventurous than their parents, so we gave them permission to find more exciting challenges, at the end of which they were to proceed together to the hotel. Audrey and I were quite content to slide gracefully down the less demanding gradients.

That was the day that Audrey learnt her first German phrase. "Meine Sonne, er ist verloren" – sob, sob. It came about in this way: - from the beginning, we had emphasized to the lads that should any one of them lose touch with the others he should make for a specific position near the upper cable station, and wait there until joined by his brothers. Also, that they were not to proceed down to the village by cable car unless they were together. One had to be queuing at the upper station by about 4pm, and it was a bit of a zoo jostling for position with Europeans of all cultural stripes using their own methods of gaining advantage. One got used to it, but it was never very pleasant. Anyway, there was apparently a bit of confusion and Chris and Michael assumed that David had made his own way down. Shortly after our own arrival in Kaprun the last cable car had disgorged its passengers and the system shut down for the night.

On arrival at the lodgings we met Christopher and Michael, but no sign whatsoever of David. We cast about anxiously searching for son no.3. It was then that Audrey mysteriously acquired her first German words - spoken I might add with some passion ---"Meine Sonne, er ist verloren" – sob, sob. She repeated this often enough to attract the attention of some members of the ski patrol. I must add that I was equally concerned, but had certainly not reached the panic stage. With commendable speed the machinery of the cable car system was started up and a search party headed for the hills and hopefully, our David. Thankfully he was indeed discovered, sitting under a cable pylon, where he insists to this day that he was told to wait. Anyway, with that bit of excitement behind us, we agreed that on the whole the trip had been a great success and resolved to return the following year.

It was after that second trip that I decided to edit and splice together the 8mm film footage I had taken, and shortly afterwards we gathered in our basement for the premier of "The Deere Family Skiers".

There is one scene of Audrey in a rather ungainly fashion sliding down a slope and attempting to negotiate a turn. She is bent forward with an expression of grim determination and is clearly not enjoying the experience. All men who wish to continue to enjoy the benefits of married bliss learn quite quickly that there is a time and place to enjoy a good chuckle, but this was not one of them. The boys were not subject to such inhibitions, and unkindly they roared with laughter. "That's it, that's it" cried my dear wife," I am NOT going skiing ever again!" and she never did.

Ports of Call
More of Bruce

It is the nature of life in an airline that on overnight layovers there is quite of lot of fraternization between the flight crew and members of the cabin crew. Notwithstanding mythology created by books such as "Coffee, Tea or Me" and public perceptions in general, the majority of any fraternisation between cabin crew and flight crew is innocuous, and lasts only until the flight lands back at home base. Of course, there are a significant number of exceptions, but broken marriages from this cause are few and far between. Also, in the fairly early days of airline operation air hostesses (as they were then called) were chosen partly for their relative youth and good looks. All that changed with the re-emergence after many years of dormancy, of women's so-called liberation, when lobby groups of all shapes and sizes successfully campaigned for women to continue employment after marriage and into late middle age. So in the period of which I am writing the flight attendants, which they had now become, were not necessarily pretty, or young, or to the chagrin of many a single pilot, willing!!

That preamble leads me to this next anecdote regarding a particular layover in Frankfurt and which features once again the "character" Bruce Warwick.

On this occasion the co-pilot and myself had agreed to meet at the usual 5pm for a noggin or two at a local pub. At the appointed hour, whilst I was waiting in the lobby for my crew-mate, two of our flight attendants appeared and accepted my invitation to join us for a pre-dinner drink or two, followed by a schnitzel or something equally nourishing. After dinner we decided to pay a visit to the well-known and frequented Oberbayern, a large beer hall on the Kaiserstrasse (The main street running through the city). This locally famous beer hall was as usual very well attended, and much Teutonic revelry was taking place, with muscular

Frauleins efficiently distributing litres of beer six at a time to the apparently parched customers. The 'Oom-Pa-Pa' band was going at full blast, accompanied by lots of singing and general hilarity.

It took some time to find seats at one of the many tables, but we eventually succeeded and ordered drinks, the quantity and nature of which are long forgotten. It was not long before a "Blumen Fraulein" appeared at our table, and I understood that she was offering flowers for us to buy for our lady companions. We rather ungallantly turned her down, but the flower seller indicated that the flowers had already been purchased and were being presented to our ladies by admirers from afar. Well, not too far. The girl pointed in the direction of a table on the other side of the hall, upon which were standing our old friend Bruce Warwick and his navigator, Gregory Minskoski. They were attempting, but not quite succeeding, a gracious bow in our direction. Courtesy demanded that we do the decent thing and join them, although knowing Bruce I was a little apprehensive as to what would happen next. They certainly appeared to have the outward appearance of moderate inebriation, but seemed in reasonable control of their senses and behaviour, and Bruce was above all a gentleman in the nicest sense of the word, so our companions were in no danger.

Bruce explained rather slowly, and with only occasional slurring of his words, that instead of "wasting the morning in bed" after arrival at the hotel, they had decided to take a cruise on the River Main They had embarked on the 10am cruise boat for a six-hour tour. In true German tradition the ship's bar was open throughout the tour, which of course was the motive for the cruise in the first place. By the time the boat docked at 4pm or thereabouts, Bruce and Gregory had each been imbibing steadily for about six hours, after an overnight flight from Toronto, and with no subsequent rest. One can only be astonished at their stamina and capacity, but by repute they both had plenty of practice.

I would have probably collapsed after the first two steins and been carried ashore in a horizontal position.

After leaving the boat, they had searched out a restaurant and enjoyed a leisurely meal, their next port of call being the Oberbayern, where they had been taking a full and enthusiastic part in the proceedings. All this was explained whilst we sipped away at our lager.

After an hour or so of their company, I decided that it was time for me to return to the hotel and hopefully have a good night's sleep in preparation for the rigours of the morrow's return to Toronto. The girls agreed, and the four of us left Bruce and Gregory to their own devices and "just one more before we turn in".

Whether they did indeed have just one is certainly open to conjecture, but in the fullness of time they left the Oberbayern and commenced the shortish stagger back to their lodgings at the prestigious five-star Hotel Intercontinental. At that time the Frankfurt council was in the process of making major changes to the city infrastructure, for just about every street in that area was partly dug up, with ditches and barriers and all the paraphernalia of construction scattered hither and thither. When Bruce and Gregory emerged from the warmth of the Oberbayern they were greeted by a blast of cold night air. Many years of hard living had long accustomed Bruce to dealing with a simple problem like getting home after a hard night out, but unfortunately Gregory was made of less stern stuff and his legs lost the ability to keep him upright. He collapsed upon the cold surface of the Kaiserstrasse. Bruce now had a problem, for taxis were hard to come by, what with the dug-up roads and the lateness of the hour. He saw the answer to his dilemma lying nearby – in the shape of a discarded wheelbarrow left near a pile of broken strasse.

About fifteen minutes later another returning pilot (without whose evidence this tale could not be recorded for posterity) witnessed the rather amusing sight of Bruce staggering along the road pushing a wheelbarrow containing his recumbent and loudly snoring Navigator. Without hesitation Bruce boldly pushed the barrow through the hotel door, walked the length of the well-appointed lobby, passing the astonished staff behind the check-in desk, and into the lift. Sadly the tale must end there, because both main characters have long sought out their maker. Perhaps the rest of the story was confided to someone still alive, but I suspect that all that is left to be told is of a mystified chambermaid wondering why she found a wheelbarrow in a room at the Frankfurt Intercontinental.

The tale of Canadian Tire

One of the most enjoyable episodes of my flying career was the five years or so I spent on the short/medium range Douglas DC9. It was a very nice aeroplane to fly, suffered very few mechanical problems, and was a relatively stress-free job once one had got used to the rather frenetic departure procedures. The DC9 needed just a two-man crew, at a time when nearly all larger aeroplanes required three or four crew members, so the business of fuelling, flight planning, passenger counts, start-up and departure procedures had to be dealt with mainly by the co-pilot, who for about fifteen minutes at the start of each trip had to work like the proverbial one-armed paper-hanger. However, after a few weeks getting used to the job, one could tackle these tasks quite efficiently.

Also, for a very pleasant change in my own life, jet-lag was no longer an issue. One often had to begin work at the crack of dawn and finish late at night, but our duty and rest hours were more or less in sync with the rest of Canadian society.

There were still plenty of layovers, but often they were just a couple of hours flying time away from base. One good example was New York, a city I had not seen much of until my posting on the DC9. We stayed downtown at the Hilton Hotel opposite Carnegie Hall and I got quite familiar with that area. I often went for breakfast just down the road from the hotel, where there would be quite a number of performers of all degrees of fame taking a break from the rigours imposed by the choreographers and other Carnegie taskmasters. Anyway, for an observer of the human condition it gave added spice to my "easy over and streaky bacon."

New York is a very interesting city and in many ways much maligned, for as far as cities go it can be just as much fun as Paris or London. Also, it was my experience that people were far more friendly that in European cities. It is quite easy to start up an amiable conversation in a bar or restaurant and people seem genuinely interested. One also meets all sorts of characters, many of whom could be the basis of a good story or novel. One of the endearing qualities of a typical New York pub is that if one appears to be intent on spending some time in the establishment, every so often the barman tops up one's glass "on the house". This certainly encourages loyalty, as do the free finger foods that can often take the place of dinner.

Speaking of food, on one rather memorable occasion a fellow named Randy and myself went out to dinner, and after a convivial evening were returning to the hotel when we were quite politely "accosted" by a coloured lady, with whom we exchanged some witticisms and pleasantries. However, we were not on the market, so to speak, and made that quite plain. Randy and I intended ending our evening with a nightcap from his overnight kit before hitting the sheets, but the lady followed us to his room and persuaded us to let her join us for a drink and a chat before she went in search of more profitable pickings. It was prime time for her and she should not have been wasting it on a couple of cheapskates like us. We had both experienced similar encounters in other American cities and it was surprising how many of the ladies of the night simply enjoyed a social chat. They also were not averse to haggling over the price should anything more intimate come up in conversation.

So we chatted about this and that for about half an hour, at which time she broached the subject of her profession and how we could help her pay the grocery bill. Both Randy and I stated unequivocally that firstly we were not interested in sex, (A bit of a fib, but certainly not with her!!) and secondly that we could not afford to indulge in such dubious pleasures. She was clearly prepared to dicker (excuse the pun) on the price, but we convinced her that we did not possess the necessary cash by displaying the contents of our wallets. I had about ten Canadian dollars (barely enough for the preliminaries to a knee-tremble), whilst Randy had five dollars Canadian and, of all things, about twenty dollars in "Canadian Tire Notes". (These are in fact merchandise coupons that resemble paper money). In spite of our apparent poverty our lady seemed inclined to linger on in our company and I was getting anxious to get to bed – alone. I therefore made my excuses and departed for my own room, where within a ten minutes I was comfortably established between the sheets and contemplating a pleasant sleep.

About half an hour later I was woken from deep slumber by someone knocking on the door. You've guessed it – it was our lady-friend, who pleaded to come in for a few minutes. I was somewhat surprised that Randy had not sent her packing long before, and I told her through the closed door that I was really not interested, and in any case, had to get some kip. However, an essential part of her professional skill was persuasion -"Please, just let me in for a few minutes. I won't stay long and I have something to ask you". Obviously, our friend was a very lonely lady of the night and if she carried on like this she would also be a very poor lonely lady of the night. Anyway, I allowed her to sit in the chair for a while and we chatted about this and that before I insisted she leave. "Oh, alright baby," or some such endearment, "but before I go could you change these for me?" and she pulled out from her purse about twenty dollars in "Canadian Tire Money".

Disturbing tales

One of the banes of the life of long-distance airline crews is of course, dealing with the dreaded jet lag and attempts to sleep during the daylight hours of the country one happens to have landed in, hopefully as planned. For instance, most of the transatlantic flying from North America to Europe takes place overnight, with scheduled arrivals in European cities in the morning or even early afternoon. One has been on the go since arising from bed on the morning of the departure city and consequently the vast majority of crew members desire nothing more than a good sleep as soon as possible after landing. Allowing for the arrival formalities and sometimes a bus ride of about an hour, one is lucky to have one's head hit the pillow much before mid-day in the host country. If conditions were right, it took me all of about two minutes to succumb to deep slumber, often to be awakened about four hours later by a more energetic fellow crew member seeking a bit of company. After a convivial drink followed by a leisurely meal it was usually time to return to our lodgings and attempt to get a good night's sleep before facing the rigours of the return to base. Anyone who has done this a few times fully understands the problems of jet lag and the difficulties of sleeping, so I will not dwell further on the subject.

A constant problem was that conditions for deep slumber during daylight hours were often far from ideal. I quickly learnt to ask for a room in the quiet part of the hotel, which often turned out to be not so quiet – with vacuum cleaners whirring away, noisy housekeeping staff blabbing with each other and umpteen other distractions. One of the frustrations upon arrival at a hotel was that the assigned rooms were not ready for occupation. This was particularly true for hotels in London, where we often suffered delays of up to two hours. I believe that the hotel staff made a sincere effort on our behalf, if only to clear the lobby area of grotty- looking crew members lolling around in the few available armchairs. Nevertheless, it was quite often a fact of life and most of us suffered in silence. There was one flight attendant whose extrovert and excitable personality certainly qualified him as a "character". He seemed to enjoy kicking up a song and dance act at the check-in desk if he was compelled to wait more than ten minutes for his room key. This provided a couple of harmless minutes of entertainment for the rest of us, but did nothing for the five-star status claimed by the hotel. On one occasion (which has since become part of Air Canada folklore) he dragged his suitcase into the lobby cloakroom, appearing a few minutes later clad in just his pyjamas, and then demanded to see the manager. A room "miraculously" became available in about a minute.

Certainly, not having a room ready upon arrival was very annoying, but even more annoying was getting to one's assigned room and hearing traffic honking and roaring past the window.

I never quite had the courage for such theatrical tactics as the above aggrieved flight attendant, but I certainly made frequent complaints about noisy rooms. It helped to get to know the manager, who usually would do his or her best to satisfy the conditions necessary for peaceful slumber in the middle of a working day. On one occasion I arrived at the hotel about midday, tired out and yearning to put my head down for a few hours. The assistant manager was on duty and assured me that my room, being away from the main road, would be peaceful. I undressed, had a quick shower, dusted myself down with some fragrant talc and duly slid between the clean sheets. I had barely put my head upon the pillow, when I became aware of a thump, thump, thump, thump, at about a hundred decibels, from somewhere just beyond my window sill. The racket ceased after a minute or so and I relaxed once more. Then ---thump, thump, thump thump. I dragged myself to the window and there below was the largest pneumatic drill (Jack Hammer) I have ever seen – really. It was more like a pile driver and was powered by some sort of diesel motor. The workmen were hard at work digging a deep hole, which they had only just started. Thump, thump -------. "ello, is that the manager. Listen to this" – and I held the telephone receiver towards the window ---thump, thump etc. "Have a look out of your bleedin' lobby window." "Oh dear sir, I am very sorry, didn't know they were going to start that job today. Would you like a quieter room?" "Too bloody right." I said, as I dragged my clothes back into my suitcase.

And so it went, one hotel after another, no matter what country I was in. I somehow seemed to attract noisy machinery wherever I went. The five-star Geneva Intercontinental was no exception. I was once woken there by the sound of a large electric drill apparently aimed at my left ear from the room next door. There again, I lifted the telephone receiver and held it to the wall for the benefit of the fellow at the front desk. A quieter room was the result, but upon my thanking the management that evening for their consideration, I was told that the drill was in fact eight floors above my own room, which implied that one electric drill could be disturbing the peace of about thirty rooms in an up-market hotel.

To add to the misery of attempting slumber during the daylight hours, occasionally there were statutory fire drills at odd times throughout the day. I once arrived at my hotel in Frankfurt to be warned by a note at my bedside that "The hotel will be carrying out a fire alarm test this afternoon and we request guests treat it as a real alarm. Please act accordingly, and on no account use the lifts". At about 2pm I was rudely awakened from deep slumber by the strident sound of the fire alarm. I shook myself awake, had a quiet conference with my conscience, and sensibly decided to honor the drill (if that's what it was). One was not supposed to linger in those circumstances, so using my airline-issue lightweight raincoat to cover my dignity, I left the room and briskly plodded my way down the emergency staircase from the fourteenth floor to the hotel lobby. On entering the lobby I was startled to see that of the thirty or so guests going about their business, I was the only one attired in just a lightweight raincoat. There was not another pair of short fat hairy legs to be seen. Whatever fire drills were being practiced elsewhere on the premises, they certainly were unaware of them here. I could easily have been mistaken for a dodgy character about to set off for the local park for the purposes of illegal display. Nothing for it, but do a smart about face and stagger back up the fourteen flights of stairs and to my room.

And it came to pass that I was asleep in my hotel in London when the fire alarm went off. It was about two o'clock in the morning, not usually the time allotted for fire drills, so this could be the real thing. In view of the previous fiasco, I lingered a few minutes wondering if it was a false alarm, and then glanced out the window. Far below was a steady stream of half dressed guests exiting the hotel, presumably to escape the inferno within. With rather more alacrity than at the Frankfurt fire drill I donned the same raincoat and trotted down the fire staircase – this time only about five floors. I crossed the lobby and joined the large crowd of hotel guests gathered in the courtyard, where we waited, shivering, with no obvious sign of a conflagration anywhere nearby. However, there *were* a couple of fire trucks and associated personnel in attendance, so clearly my journey was not in vain. In the fullness of time we were advised that we could wait in the lobby, but not return to our rooms. Apparently, a kitchen appliance of some sort had caused the problem. Anyway, I made myself comfortable in an armchair and for the first time glanced at some of my fellow sufferers. It appeared that I had intruded upon a Halloween gathering of some sort, for there were some authentic-looking witches and ghouls sitting around, looking rather sleepy. There was something familiar about the nearest witch, whose face was covered by a thick white mask, with her hair in a sort of cage of netting. After a closer inspection I realized that my conjecture regarding All

Hallows Eve was probably in error, for she was in fact one of Air Canada's senior flight attendants, dressed strictly for solitary repose. I looked around and saw at least two other members of our cabin crew dressed in a somewhat similar fashion. It was not a pretty sight, and I rather unkindly commented afterwards that, in the event of future fire alarms, would it not be preferable to risk being consumed by fire than have our senior staff suffer the embarrassment of being seen in their war-paint. Not that us fellows were anything to write home about, but most of us chose not to resort to engineering and mudpacks to improve our appearance.

So you can see that the glamour of airline flying is not all that it is cracked up to be. In the early years after retirement I suffered a few bouts of nostalgia regarding my past career, but these feelings were quickly dispelled by going through in my mind all the stages of a transatlantic trip, including possible fire alarms, noisy rooms and waking up for the day's work having achieved just a couple of hours sleep. The only things I really missed were the undoubted comradeship, the beer --- and the money.

Back to Ireland

In the mid eighties I was employed on the Tri-Star L1011 airliner. It was a bit of a workhorse and was used on the long-range routes as far as Singapore, as well as what was essentially holiday charters across the ocean or down to the Caribbean. Subsequently it was replaced by the Boeing 747, but of the two, flying the Tri-Star was more interesting for me, for we had a far more varied route structure, including a few summers when we flew charters to Shannon. The Shannon flight schedule included a one-night layover in the town of Limerick, where we were comfortably accommodated at Jury's Hotel. Limerick is my kind of town, (apologies to Frankie boy!) in that it is a small country town with everything important for a layover: -- pubs, restaurants and hotels, all within reasonable staggering distance of each other. Also the inhabitants were very friendly, providing one did not present a dissenting view of "The Troubles"

I flew a number of these flights and got to know the place quite well. Sometime in the late eighties a lad named Ian Clark, who was, and still is, a good friend of my son, gained national fame as a junior champion cross-country runner. He was entered into the Junior World Cross-Country Championship to be held, in all places, Limerick, Ireland. A number of his close chums, including my son Christopher, decided to be there in support, and they made the necessary travel plans. I had very little input into these arrangements and had no intention of joining the group, so they had good reason to believe that in Ireland they would be well beyond parental scrutiny. However, by sheer chance I was drafted for a flight to Shannon on the day after their departure. We arrived at Jury's Hotel about 10am the following morning and I was soon between the sheets sleeping off the overnight flight. I woke up at about 3pm and, after a cup of tea, took a stroll through the town. Not long after leaving the hotel I glanced across the street and saw son Chris with Ian and about four other obviously high-spirited youths, behaving as young people do when their parents are three-thousand miles away. I commenced to cross the road at about the same time as they decided to do the same. Being well into middle age I was of course invisible to most young people, and this was no exception, until I said, "Hello, Chris". Their shock and surprise was a joy to behold, and one of them shook his head in obvious disbelief, and perhaps chagrin. A spy! Anyway, after they had recovered, I took them into a local café for a cup of tea and a chat. The race had been that day and Ian had come in third – an excellent result for Ian and Canada. Sadly, his promising athletic career was cut short by bothersome leg injuries. He is now a senior civil servant and doing very well. I had no intention of interfering with their plans and, apart from a convivial beer in the evening with Chris and one of his pals, I left them to their own devices. In any case, I was flying the group back to Canada the following day.

Apparently, some time later that evening they returned to the race venue and succeeded in "rescuing" the large banner across the course advertising the "1984 World Junior Cross Country Championships, Limerick" The banner was about 4 feet high by about 50 feet long. They somehow managed to stagger back to their hotel with their booty and the following morning took it as part of their baggage. A large roll of material about three feet in diameter does not really fit a passenger agent's idea of personal baggage, and there was a bit of a fuss trying to convince the passenger agent to accept it without incurring charges. Chris piped up with the obvious solution –"It's okay, my Dad's flying the aeroplane", which cut absolutely no ice with the agent. However, she called our operations manager, (I believe it was Brendan, the fellow who once mislaid my ticket – page 38). He came along, took one look at the large roll of material, quickly put two and two together and exclaimed "You thievin' little buggers. You've pinched that from Limerick racecourse!" all of which was perfectly true. But of course being a good- hearted Irishman, he took charge of the contraband and it was duly put into the hold, no charge. I knew nothing of this exchange until I reported to the office to do the flight planning. By that time he had arranged for a cameraman to take a Public Relations picture of the First Officer and his thieving son. Sadly, I have never set eyes on the picture.

God Save the who?

During August 1985 I was lucky enough to be assigned three Shannon layovers, therefore becoming quite familiar with Limerick and able to establish a nice routine that ensured pleasant walks, good beer when needed and a nourishing and relatively inexpensive meal, followed, of course, by a good night's sleep preparatory to the return to Toronto with another load of returning Paddies. The only snag was that evening of the layover was on a Saturday, when the local populace was competing for pub and restaurant space, so it was wise to stake an early claim for one's choice in the restaurant. On one occasion there were five of us seated quite early in the evening and being a keen observer of the human condition, I took some interest in my fellow diners. In the main, they seemed to be farming folk in town for the evening, and no doubt their next port of call after the meal was their favourite pub. Anyway, on this particular evening we were lucky to find a very nice steakhouse, where both the food and the service were of a good standard.

After the meal we left the restaurant and in the normal course of affairs would have returned to the hotel for a nightcap before hitting the hay. However, on our way to our hotel we came across a club that advertised that Paddy O'Hara and his pieces of Five (or some such title) were playing, and membership was available to all. Worth a try. We entered the premises, paid the entrance fee, and found ourselves within what I remembered from half a century before as a good old-fashioned dance hall. They still exist in some parts of the globe. We found ourselves a table next to the dance floor and settled down with pints of Guinness for the chaps and white wine for the ladies, and spent a convivial few hours enjoying the proceedings. 'Twas all quite decorous and above board, and I was quite happy to sit there sipping my brew, watching the local Irish lads shaking a huff with the lasses. Time went by and it seemed to me that Last Waltz time was almost upon us. The band struck up another tune and, rather to my surprise it seemed that everyone had a sudden urge to dance, so on impulse I took the hand of the nearest lady and began to show off my fancy footwork. All I got for my efforts was an alarmed look as she exclaimed, "Stand still you fool – it's the National Anthem!"

Not long after midnight we arrived back at the hotel and I soon repaired to my quarters, had a good soak in the bath and went to bed. I was very tired. Maybe I was overtired, for I woke up in the early hours and was tossing and turning, hoping to drop off once more into slumber. My eyes wandered aimlessly around the room and settled on what appeared to be a large round flowerpot on the window-sill. I had not noticed it before, but who takes much notice of hotel room furnishings? For no reason I can think of, I studied it for a few moments, and to my surprise, it seemed to move its position. An optical illusion brought on by fatigue? However, it seemed to sprout eyes and a nose and moved again, and I realized that I was staring at a human head. My instinctive response was an alarmed yelp and the head magically disappeared, followed by the sound of running footsteps. I leaped from bed, rushed to the window, but whoever it was had faded into the night. My room was on the 2nd floor of the hotel, so it was rather mysterious, for there was no ladder or fire escape nearby. I woke up the night porter, who awakened the manager, who alerted the constabulary. Apparently the police were already aware that a pair of petty thieves was on the prowl in Limerick, one standing on the other's shoulders to get to the upstairs windows. How successful they were I shall never know, but I always think of that episode as "The night the flowerpot moved".

Portuguese adventure

This is the tale of our first and only trip to Portugal. The airline TAP had for some time been offering airline employees a discounted fare of $90 return from Montreal to Lisbon. If I recall correctly, it was called the Navigator Fare (not meant to acknowledge my own credentials but a predecessor ---- Vasco-de-Whatsisname).

After a little research, Audrey and I decided that Lisbon would be a suitable starting point for a couple of weeks in the Algarve, in Southern Portugal, followed by a week or so in Normandy, where it had long been my ambition to visit the D-Day Beaches. We would also take in the famous tapestry at Bayeaux and tour that part of France. By now the boys were well able to spend a couple of weeks without parental control, so we felt little guilt as we set forth for the airport. First, we had to get to Montreal's Dorval airport via Air Canada's Rapidair service -- the rapid bit assuming one could get there with a standby ticket. In anticipation of success I checked the bags in and we waited patiently at the gate as the planned aeroplane filled up to the gunwales with paying passengers, leaving us sitting in the departure lounge in the hope of getting on the following flight, which in the fullness of time also went rapidly on its way without us. We had a dilemma:- it was by now too late to catch the Lisbon flight, which left from Mirabel Airport and involved a half-hour transfer from Dorval, but we did have the option of taking the British Airways flight to London and flying down to Faro (our final destination) from there. The only snag was that our luggage had not been denied boarding at Toronto and was, by now, getting very dizzy going round and round on the luggage carousel in Montreal awaiting our arrival. Using a bit of initiative, I telephoned the Pilot Crew Room in Montreal and persuaded a presumably recumbent pilot awaiting his next tasked flight, to find our bags and put 'em on the next Rapidair to Toronto. This is obviously long before various liberation armies made such informal arrangements impossible as well as illegal. Those were much more insouciant days and how I miss them. Fortunately, our bags arrived back in Toronto in time for us to be boarded on the London flight. I had used the waiting time to purchase standby tickets from London to Faro, where we should be arriving late afternoon on the following day – not too much delayed by the new arrangements.

Sadly our plans were once again thwarted, when our London aeroplane developed a technical problem, causing a delay of about ninety minutes. This made its revised arrival time at London about half an hour *after* the departure time of our Faro flight. However, on arrival at London we found that it was a bad time for technical snags on British Airways flights, and to our relief the Faro bound machine was still in London undergoing repairs, so we could, after all, continue on to Portugal that day. By the time we did depart from London, it was clear we would arrive in Faro at about midnight, but without any local currency or arrangements for a hotel. I had intended doing all that on arrival in Lisbon in what should have been normal office hours. Midnight in some remote outpost of the Iberian Peninsular was a much different proposition.

The terminal building in Faro turned out to be a converted hangar in which services appeared to be minimal, and the lateness of the hour ensured that most of these were closed, including currency exchange facilities and the hotel booking agency. To add to these problems, there were at least three hundred very excitable Portuguese looking for a ride into town. The few taxis available were in massive demand and I was reminded yet again (try Austrian ski hills for a display of discourtesy and queue jumping) that the reputed courtesy of Europeans is but a myth.

There was a taxi rank of sorts, around which were gathered a large crowd of pushing, shoving and voluble Portuguese. The "technique" used to obtain a taxi was to leap madly into the road ahead of an arriving vehicle and grab one of its door handles before it had come to a stop. I learned that it is possible for about six otherwise sane adults to grab the same door handle, so for a four-door vehicle, there were at least twenty-four aggressive Latinos attempting to commandeer each cab. How the hell any of them actually managed to enter the vehicle is still a mystery. This was a situation with which Audrey and I were totally unfamiliar and, after a few desultory attempts to join the mob, we gave up and hoped for someone in authority to come to the rescue. We were in luck, for a local gendarme had been observing this madhouse and decided to take matters into his own hands.

He shouted a few words in the local tongue, presumably politely, asking folks to take their proper turn, but to no avail. He then managed to get the madding crowd's undivided attention by the rather simple expedient of pulling his revolver from its holster and in no uncertain terms, ordering them to get back into line. This certainly gave another meaning to " Terminal Building", but to our relief it worked, and we were soon on our way into town, accompanied by another Canadian couple with whom we had agreed to share the lift. There were now just two snags left in this long journey from Toronto to Faro: - firstly, I did not have the wherewithal to pay my share of the taxi fare, and secondly, if and when I overcame that problem I had no idea where we would sleep. Our companions suggested that we all went to their hotel and I could pay them what I owed for the taxi on the following day. Our companions' lodgings were in fact a bed and breakfast and the owner regretfully informed us that he was fully booked. His eyes then lit up with inspiration. With sign language and limited English he indicated that he could have one room available if we would be so good as to give him half an hour or so to arrange things.

Remember, this was in the early hours of the morning. A few minutes later a very disgruntled old lady, wrapped in a presumably hastily donned shawl, squeezed past, gave us a very dirty look and went off muttering loudly into some other part of the dwelling. It was reasonable to presume that Mother-in-law had been turfed from her bed and told to go elsewhere. Fifteen minutes or so later we were thankfully settled into a newly made bed from which emanated just a hint of lavender and the warm human glow of a previous incumbent.

      The following ten days or so went very well, but I shall not bore the reader with an amateur travelogue except for my brief reminiscence of my first venture on to a 'nudie' beach. I had been wandering along the beach looking for shells and other interesting flotsam and jetsam, when from the corner of my eye I became aware of a sunbather just a few feet away. I looked up and prepared to offer a friendly greeting, but to my embarrassment my gaze was directed at a bare bosom of impressive dimensions. No doubt the owner of the shapely breasts did not mind, but I quickly averted my gaze (honestly!) and in doing so became conscious of the fact that I had blundered into a sort of minefield of bare breasts and buttocks. I directed my gaze upwards at the clear blue sky and it was in that idiotic attitude that I made my escape to the more traditional environs of the adjacent beach. Since then, of course, I have witnessed such unfettered nature in all parts of the globe and I now have no qualms in having a "butchers" at nude female sunbathers. After all, they are there to be seen, probably not by me, but that's their bad luck. However, I do draw the line at the sight of two teams of naked men enthusiastically playing volleyball, seemingly unaware of the pendulous activity occurring below their waists --there should be a law against that. The first time I saw that gruesome sight was at the inappropriately name Englischer Gardens in Munich.

-- and on to France

This necessitated a flight from Faro to Lisbon and thence to Paris on the Portuguese airline TAP. Their Pilots must have had prior notice of our plans, for on our scheduled departure date they decided that they were not being paid enough escudos, and downed Control Columns. The only alternative was to travel by train to Lisbon and thence hopefully via Air France to Paris. The train journey made a very pleasant change and, of course, allowed us to see a bit more of Portugal. On arrival at Lisbon we sought out a very nice five-star hotel at a bargain rate, and a far cry from dragging grandma from her bed.

The following morning we turned up at the airport in the hope of taking an Air France plane to Paris. If we had thought our arrival at Faro was chaotic, it was nothing compared to the shambles that greeted us at the Lisbon airport departure building. It was packed with frustrated customers, most of whom obviously hadn't paid much attention to their newspapers or television news, for there were hundreds of them lined up at the check-in desks, nearly all of them shouting and shoving with absolutely no chance of getting on an aeroplane that day.

Audrey and I took our place in the queue for the Air France, Paris desk, where things were not much better, but at least there was a hope - a very slim one - of getting to Paris, for the Air France pilots had uncharacteristically decided not to come out in sympathy. The queues were just as chaotic and bad tempered as elsewhere, and we were treated to a bit of entertainment as two excited Latinos exchanged blows. In spite of the chaos, we decided to wait an hour or so and see what transpired. What transpired was bugger-all, but we were patient and polite and waited, ignoring the histrionics surrounding us. This stiff upper lip attitude paid off, for after about half and hour the hapless passenger agent manning the desk unexpectedly waved in our direction and asked us to come forward. I suppose he reasoned that two people standing quietly and without fuss were either dead or British. I explained that we were mere employee standby passengers and were there just on the off chance. "Well, you can see what it's like by looking around you, so there is little chance of you getting off today". "However, why don't you go to our office upstairs and put your name on the list for a flight deck seat?"

That was an idea I hadn't even considered. They certainly did not allow it in Canada. "But I have my wife with me", I replied. "Give it a try anyway, you won't get out of Lisbon otherwise", he said, and so we took the lift as directed and sought out the "fellow upstairs", who greeted us with great charm and courtesy, with the minor discouragement that he didn't hold out a hope in hell that we would get to Paris that day. Anyway, he very kindly put our names at the bottom of what seemed to be a long list and we returned to the departure hall, where I looked around once more at the ill-tempered mob and decided that another night in that comfortable hotel was the better alternative.

We lugged our luggage to the kerbside, hailed a taxi without armed assistance, and started loading the luggage. I suddenly became aware that a Mr. Deere was being paged on the public address system. I trotted over to the check-in desk, where an agent was waiting somewhat impatiently. "Come with me", he said. "Where to?" I asked. "To zee aeroplane" he responded. I sprinted back to the taxi, retrieved luggage and wife, and together we were ushered through the terminal hinterland and out on to the tarmac, up the stairs of an Air France aeroplane and into the flight deck, where we received a surprisingly warm welcome --. And that is how Audrey and I got to 'gay Paree'. What influence had been set in motion I have no idea, but with today's security and bureaucratic controls we have sadly seen the last of such improvised arrangements.

On arrival in Paris we hired a car and headed for Normandy and Brittany, and from there until we arrived back in Toronto there were no further accommodation or travel problems worthy of comment. There is but one more tale to tell of that trip (part true and part fantasy) -- and using poetic licence I set it to verse, so here with very fond memories of that few weeks in Portugal and France is:

A Bidet tale

Among the highlights of our visit to France were our trips to the Normandy beaches and our study of the Bayeaux Tapestry. We then traveled to Brittany and visited the quaint island of Mont. St. Michel, where we stayed in a hotel in which the rooms were once used as monks' cells. Everything was very "compact", including the toilet facilities. The bidet was tucked away under the washbasin and was wheeled out when required. After our return, I speculated in doggerel as to what might have happened had the bidet broken loose from its moorings. Our hotel was indeed half way up a steep hill, at the bottom of which was a restaurant claiming a Michelin star. To be even mentioned in the Michelin Guide means that the restaurant is of very high standard. Here then, with apologies to my dear wife for repeatedly making her the "butt" of my perverse idea of humour, is the tale of the portable bidet. (The next to last verse refers to her hobby of Rug Hooking).

On the coast of Brittany, jutting out into the sea,
Stands an old and famous Monk's Retreat.
Now, instead of meditation there is tourist exploitation,
And ecclesiastic gents no more you'll meet.

Those Monks have given way to the tourist trade today,
There are picture postcards, guided tours instead.
The old monastic cells are converted to hotels,
And in each room a venerable Bidet.

Yes, I know its boring stuff; and I've said enough,
No travelogue to you will I relate.
This concerns that white appliance on which those Gauls place great reliance,
You've guessed it, -- it is the French Bidet.

Each night we took our chance with those hotels in Northern France,
We often had a very pleasant view,
And those chambres big or small, the one thing common to them all,
Was that porcelain emplacement in the loo.

Now us British often question, the need for such a crude invention,
We are satisfied that we have greater minds,
But give credit to those Gauls, for that's where the acclaim falls,
What better way to wash their French behinds.

So at Mont Saint Michel we found a small hotel,
Its aspect was a pleasing panorama,
All was peaceful and serene as we viewed that pleasant scene,
What a contrast to the coming drama.

Our room was rather nice, comfy bed, no sign of mice,
But a rather compact closet in the place.
It was sad to say, but true, that in that tiny loo,
For the Bidet there was very little space.

The ingenious solution to this very French ablution,
Was to mobilise its static situation.
With flexi-hose and wheels and clever little seals,
When not in use it slid beneath the basin.

Now Aud's inclined to panic when faced with things mechanic,
Still, in this case she showed a brave backside.
But as she squatted to its use, a vital nut broke loose,
And across the floor the thing began to glide.

With squeaking wheels and muffled roar, the whole shebang went out the door,
I tried to catch it but it was to fast.
Poor Aud was now quite firmly in, upon her face a silly grin,
As passers by stared at the show, aghast.

That Bidet with its precious cargo, resembling an oversized escargot,
Went through those streets with uncanny ease.
A local drunk was knocked aside, he blinked and then he cried,
"Its our Lady" and sank upon his knees.

At the bottom of the hill stands a very well known Grill,
Famous for its vintage wine and crepes.
It is named in Michelin, oh my, there was a din,
As Audrey Deere came crashing through the drapes.

That elegant café overlooks the sea,
A window gives a panoramic view.
Through that expensive glass did that china toilet pass,
And so was launched the good ship 'Water Loo'.

It settled down quite fine, just above Aud's Plimsoll
Line,
My dear wife seemed to take it all quite well.
I shouted "Let go Fore" - but I think she let go Aft,
For suddenly that vessel went like hell!

It was quickly lost from sight, oh my, what a plight,
The whole darned episode was shocking.
That evening's 'dejeuner', was quite hard to put away,
With Audrey out there somewhere on the Oggin'.

But I was quickly reassured that by the morn she
would be moored,
Please do not live in fear or trepidation.
"For our Bidets are built well. They can take an
ocean swell"
"And in any case she's got built-in flotation".

That long night passed away and so dawned another day,
I joined the small crowd waiting at the quay.
And in the sunrise golden glow, we spotted Audrey
on the "Po',
An awesome sight I think you will agree.

She moored that Twyford fashioned basin, right
against the harbour caisson,
And stepped from the sea that very nearly took her.
A slightly wild look in her eye, she uttered a defiant cry,
"It takes more than that to shake this Rugged Hooker!"

There's little more to tell, I haven't told it well,
But these words of wisdom you should heed.
When you visit France, with those Bidets take no
chance,
Papier's the only thing you'll need.

One advantage of Radio Silence

In the early forties and until quite recent times there existed on the Atlantic a number of Ocean Weather Stations which had the task of assisting transatlantic flights in the form of weather reports, navigation assistance and to provide help in emergency situations. They were located at fixed locations on the Atlantic and their assigned positions were shown on the navigation charts for those areas. They must have had some sort of crew relief system, the nature about which I have no idea, but it is reasonable to assume that the crews would be changed at intervals of weeks, if not months. It was probably a tiresome and somewhat lonely existence. Among other equipment the ships had a radio beacon that was very useful in fixing the aircraft position if the flight was within about fifty miles of their location. The only snag there was that the ship's navigator was sometimes a little careless in keeping the vessel's position exactly where it was supposed to be, which could give rise to occasional navigational confusion to us up there trying to keep the aeroplane from straying far from the beaten track. However Ocean Weather Stations served an essential purpose and we were somewhat comforted by their presence on the 'oggin'. In order to relieve our, and their, boredom we often exchanged pleasantries, and one evening I was witness to the following exchange:

"Ocean Station Charlie, this is Pan Am 123, are your reading me?"

"Loud and clear, Pan Am, go ahead your message"

A female voice then comes on the air (long before there were female airline pilots)

"Hello Ocean Station Charlie, I'm a flight attendant -just like to wish you a good evening"

"Oh, Hi, Pan Am lady, lovely to chat with you. Where's your home"

"I live in Yonkers, New York, how about you?"

"What a coincidence, I will be back at my home in New York next month, perhaps we could get together for a drink, or something. What's your phone number? "

"It is 900 555 3421, but please keep it to yourself"

"Great, may see you next month"

"Pan Am 123 this is Delta 456, thanks for that, I'll give you a call"

"This is Air Canada 956, many thanks".

"This is Lufthansa 004 – vee will meet one day ven our flight is over"

"Mama Mia, loverly lady, this is Alitalia, hope to see you soon."

--- and so on. – I promise you this is a true tale somewhat paraphrased.

Caveat Emptor

Flight attendants are drawn from all walks of life and within their ranks are people of great intelligence and charm. It is true that recent legislation has allowed many of them to be employed long after they should have taken up some less demanding line of work, but that applies to a small minority. Also, it is a myth that there is a preponderance of homosexuals among the male flight attendants. I was however once greeted by a middle-aged male flight attendant, who confided quietly to me that there was a Queer in the crew. "Oh" I replied cautiously, "Who is it?" "Kiss me and I'll tell you", he responded.

As most flight attendants will tell you, among the main reasons for them to apply for the job was the opportunity to see other parts of the world, and access to shopping opportunities not available at home, and this leads me on to the next tale.

One of the advantages of working on the international routes rather than flying just within North America is that literally a whole new world opened up when it came to shopping opportunities. For those laying over in London there was Oxford Street with many flight attendants heading straight for the delights of Marks and Spencer's, or famous Selfridges, which is just next door. What I still do not understand is that many of the girls were senior enough go to London once a week for up to a year, and on almost each occasion they seemed to head straight for Marks and Spencer's It is a complete mystery to me what on earth they found so interesting after the first two visits. . (I have just consulted with my female "advisor" and she has responded that it is possible to enjoy visiting that famous store for every week of one's life and not run out of ideas). In the eighties the same ladies successfully bid to fly to Bombay and Singapore, thus opening up a cornucopia of shopping choices. Both those places were great for having made-to-measure garments delivered just a few hours after they were chosen. However, the results did not always quite fulfil the promises made on quality and fit. A good friend of mine once held a party at his home in Montreal. The only stipulation was that one had to wear a shirt tailored in Bombay, and which had been washed --- once!

My favourite "shopping disaster" story concerns a young lady who took a liking to the exotic and expensive Persian carpets in a particular Bombay shop. The shop was, and possibly still is, located in the Oberoi Hotel, Bombay, and thus carried with it the prestige of the hotel itself. She splurged the princely sum of about three thousand Canadian dollars on a beautiful carpet measuring about five feet by three feet, and proudly carried it back to Toronto, where it was put to work inviting the admiration of visitors to her home. One of those visitors suggested that she have it properly insured, and so she took it for appraisal to a Toronto carpet dealer. The appraiser studied it for just a few minutes and assessed its worth at about three hundred dollars. She was not exactly "gruntled" with this alarming news and the rug accompanied her back to Bombay on her next trip in that direction. She went through all sorts of bother trying to get a refund, and finally settled for three hundred dollars a month, and that was after threats to the dealer from various higher authorities.

If one pays in dollars one can get only rupees back, and only then in exceptional circumstances. So it pays to be very, very careful when dealing with our Eastern brethren. Having said that, I still have a couple of items purchased in Bombay over twenty years and they continue to serve me well.

Distant Friends

My departure from the Royal Air Force coincided with a general exodus from that fine service of many of the colleagues and friends with whom I had served for much of my service career. Naturally we kept contact in civilian life and many of them had, like me, departed British shores for careers elsewhere. One thing people in the aircrew trades have to accept is that they cannot be too choosy about where to pursue their career. Consequently, many of my old squadron mates were now living far from their native shore, but the upside of that is that they were well rewarded both financially and in the opportunities available to their children.

The years went by, and there came the time when the family had left the nest and Mum and Dad could venture further afield, in the course of which to visit some of those old chums. Our first trip of this kind was to New Zealand, with an excursion of about four days to Melbourne (to visit my old friend, Peter Barnet), and then up to Brisbane for a further week, where one of the bridesmaids at our wedding had made her home. Our three weeks in New Zealand simply flashed by as we toured that wonderful country, visiting family and friends along our chosen route. A very good friend from our Singapore days saw us off from Auckland on the next leg of our travels – to Melbourne, Australia. This was in the days before the Internet became useful for booking hotels, and I had written a short note to Peter requesting that he find a reasonable hotel for our three-day visit. Many readers will know through bitter experience that it is a mistake to assume that one's friends are familiar with the hotels in their area of domicile. Come to think of it, there is no reason why they should. Peter did his best, except that he didn't actually *visit* the chosen hotel. To cut a long story short, we arrived at the hotel in late evening and to our dismay the only room available appeared to be a badly converted boiler room, with paint flaking from the walls and exposed air ducts across the ceiling. Peter's wife, Nicky, was mortified, and suggested we find somewhere else, but we decided to put up with it for one night and look for better digs the following day. We had a snack in a nearby café and shortly afterwards retired for the night. We were woken from sound slumber by a loud knocking on the door. I looked at my watch. It was 12.30am. Who could it possibly be at such a late hour? None other than the night clerk.

"Excuse me sir, would you please step outside for a moment".

I stepped outside.

"Yer credit card's no good, so you'll have to pay me cash".

"But we don't have any Aussie money, or much money of any currency come to that".

"Well, cobber", (he had dispensed with the "Sir" at the first hint of penury), "you'd better find some or you and yer missus can find other lodgings".

"What's wrong with my credit card?" I asked.

"Don't know mate, but it's not accepted".

He waited rather impatiently whilst I phoned the Sydney agency dealing with Visa credit cards, and sure enough, the lady informed me that my card was not valid. Well, it bloody-well had been valid in New Zealand, I told her, but to no avail. The long and the short of it was that Audrey and I managed to scrape together enough bits of various currencies to afford the flea-pit for that night, and we promptly returned to bed in the hope that there would be no more interruptions to our sleep.

The following day I told Peter of our predicament, but as he had not seen me for a number of years he was not too inclined to be much help in the finance department. The local banks were useless, so we took a chance and checked in at one of the best hotels in Melbourne. I crossed my fingers that they would not check the validity of my card and fortunately, that was the case. We were now comfortably accommodated, but being without ready cash, had to rely on our dodgy credit card, which thankfully was accepted for routine purchases. It was a holiday weekend back in Canada, so I had to wait until the following Tuesday before the matter was resolved after a fifteen minute wait, listening to pop music at about a dollar per minute, followed by a short conversation with the Visa lady in Toronto, who told me that my card was perfectly okay. What had happened I have no idea, but I promptly put the card to the test by (successfully) withdrawing some cash from a nearby bank, and from then on we had no further bother. My sons later gave me the moral of the story, "Well Dad, you've got to have at least two cards with you". – yet another example of "out of the mouths of babes!"

  We enjoyed the visit immensely and, after the allotted four days, set forth for Brisbane and our old bridesmaid, or to put it more delicately, our bridesmaid of old, Julie. She also was not familiar with local hostelries and, like Peter, had consulted the Yellow Pages and booked us a room in a hotel she had never set eyes upon.

  Many readers will know that the majority of Aussie pubs dignify their name by freely using the word "hotel" to describe the establishment, which is really there for the sole purpose of dedicated drinking, with perhaps a few rooms attached to cater for patrons who are incapable of leaving the premises. Julie had booked us into such an establishment. There was nothing wrong with it for its designated purpose, but it was *not* a hotel in accordance with the Trade Descriptions Act. The receptionist/barman who greeted us at the pub was friendly and showed us to our room. It was certainly far better than what had greeted us upon our Melbourne arrival, but within a few seconds a large diesel lorry roared past the window, followed by a second and then a third! I didn't hear the fourth or fifth, for I was on my way downstairs to consult with the management.

  "Sorry, mate, but that's the only room available".

Then he thought for a few seconds, -- "Unless you'd like the room without windows".

"What!" I exclaimed. "You can't be serious".
"Would I tell a lie, mate? We have that one room left, take it or leave it, but it's nice and cosy and you won't hear diesel lorries thundering past".

He gave us the key and we trotted upstairs and down a long corridor to the room, put the key in the lock-- and stepped into total darkness. Outside the building the sun was shining brightly. After groping around the walls, I found the light switch and the room was immediately illuminated with all the light that the single forty-watt bulb could produce. On one wall there was a set of drawn curtains, which seemed to contradict the idea of no windows. I drew one of the curtains aside and sure enough, there was indeed a large window, but right against it was a solid brick wall, with not a glimmer showing anywhere. However, the room was quite clean and, as with our first night in Melbourne, we agreed to stay just one night.

We slept surprisingly well and when we awoke our watches indicated that it was 6.30am, so by the time we had washed and dressed, the restaurant, which was in the adjacent building, should be open. We were quite peckish and wasted no time abluting and donning OZ Standard dress (shirt and shorts for me and posh summer frock for Audrey). We made our way downstairs and out into the street. No diesel lorries that time of the morning and come to that, no people at all. The restaurant was closed, but the sign on the door indicated that it opened at 7am, which was the time shown on our watches. It was warm and sunny so we didn't mind waiting a few minutes. After about fifteen minutes there was still no sign of life within the restaurant, and the street was still quite deserted. It was then that I experienced a distinct feeling of unease. Without a word to Audrey, I returned to the hotel lobby and consulted the large clock above the desk. The little hand was on the five, and the big hand pointed to a quarter past the hour.

Audrey was not too pleased to be informed that we had to find a way to pass the time for the two hours until the restaurant opened. Such are the problems of ever-changing time zones.

We had no trouble finding better lodgings, and the rest of our stay in Brisbane went very well. Brisbane was a much quieter and nicer city than it is today. They had not yet begun erecting the architectural monstrosities that now dwarf the beautiful neo-classical buildings that once made the city one of the nicest in the country. As people keep telling me with ever less conviction – that's progress.

In those days, Brisbane, along with just about every other city in Australia, shut down tight after midday on Saturdays. The streets were mostly deserted and the shops closed. It was on such a Saturday that Audrey and I stood near the beautiful Treasury building, waiting for a bus. There were just the two of us to begin with, when along came a party of about five very pretty young Asian ladies, obviously dressed up to attend a wedding. The young lady we assumed to be the bride was wearing a lovely full-length costume and carried a bouquet. We assumed her companions were her bridesmaids. After a few minutes two shiny black limousines pulled up at the curbside, and from the front of the leading car emerged a rather elderly gentleman, nattily dressed in a brown pin-stripe suit, a carnation on the lapel. He did not appear to enjoy good health, for he needed the assistance of a walking stick and his breathing seemed rather laboured. He limped towards the blushing (or was it rouge?) bride, and it soon became clear that these two were soon to be joined in some sort of matrimony (we were unable to establish whether it would be holy or secular). The difference in their ages was not so much a gap as a chasm. Of course, we had no idea of the facts, but it is probable that the bride-to-be was there in response to an advertisement in the "Manila Gazette" or some such newspaper. So we were witnessing a mail-order bride about to set forth on the adventure of a lifetime.

Luckily for her, his lifetime was much nearer its close than was hers. I don't really know what my dear wife was thinking of it all, but she perhaps spotted an inadvertent gleam in my eye. Her only comment was "Don't even think about it!" And then our bus came.

Moving at ground level

One aspect of our airline life that we tended to take for granted was the provision of ground transportation when away from home base. It could be extremely aggravating to find after a long overnight flight, that there was a delay of some sort in getting us to the hotel. And of course it was essential that we were at the airport in plenty of time for the scheduled flight departure. All this required good planning, as well as ensuring that contracts were awarded to reputable taxi or bus firms. I have already described my little shambles at Shannon Airport, Ireland, but that sort of thing was quite a rare occurrence, and I do not recall many flights that were delayed due to ground transport problems.

I was once (and only once) directly responsible for a delay at Saskatoon, when I had overlooked the fact that Saskatchewan is the only province in Canada that does not observe Daylight Saving Time, and ordered the taxi to pick us up an hour later than was required by the schedule. Luckily for us, the hotel receptionist used her own car to rush us to the airport, through airport security and to the foot of the aircraft steps, where we boarded the aircraft under the baleful eyes of those passengers who could see us slinking through the front door of the aeroplane. (That was long before current restrictive security procedures)

At our home base we were of course responsible for our own arrangements, but we did expect to return to the same airfield we had departed from at the beginning of the duty cycle. Many moons ago, an Air France Boeing 747 captain took off from Charles de Gaulle airport, Paris, and flew to New York. Two days later he was on the return journey when airline operations instructed him to land at Paris Orly. "My car is at Charles de Gaulle and that is where I am landing" was his pithy response, and that is what he did. It was a rather expensive decision for him, for I understand he sacrificed a couple of month's pay.

I have fond memories of the bus driver at Frankfurt who kept a case of cool beer in the bus icebox, exclusively for the use of incoming flight crews. We paid for them of course, but it was certainly a nice touch on a warm summer morning when we were hot and tired. But the taxi driver who gets the prize for my most amusing memory was born and bred in Glasgow. However, the tale really begins about a thousand miles to the southwest of Bonnie Scotland.

I understand that all those of the Jewish persuasion, wherever in the world they live, have automatic citizenship of the Promised Land. No doubt they have to be able to prove that they are true descendants of Jacob, or have inherited their religious adherence via a long ancestral line, but once that is established they have ready access to modern Israel. The only other country I can think of with such easy access is Canada, where it seems that the only condition of entry is to prove you are not Christian. I believe that the city of Toronto can boast about one hundred and forty (not a misprint) different ethnic groups. I haven't yet seen a genuine Pigmy, but I am working on it.

Anyway, some years ago a splendid fellow by the name of Hez Shabtai made the bold decision to move from the Promised Land to the land promised to everyone else. When I met him he was a second officer on the Lockheed L1011 Tri-Star. He speaks with a slight accent and I imagine that he had to learn the English language after his arrival. However, his mastery of the new language is not far short of his undoubted eloquence in Hebrew and I never saw him stumble over a word or difficult phrase.

He and I, along with a splendid chap named Glen McLarty were together for the month of August 1984, during which we flew charters from Toronto to Glasgow Airport. It was the same schedule every week and upon arrival at Glasgow, we were required to travel about 30 miles by taxi to our hotel near Prestwick, out of which airport we would fly the return flight to Toronto. A fairly undemanding schedule, with a very nice location for a layover and working with a very good crew -- about the best working conditions one could wish for. There was only one minor snag.

It turned out that we were to be assigned the same taxi driver every week He drove a rather nice Volvo, which he was very keen to demonstrate could achieve about 130 mph on the open road. In fact most "open roads" in that part of Scotland have their fair share of bends and narrow sections, for they are but the development of cart tracks of not so long ago. Our driver got us to the hotel near Prestwick in about twenty-five minutes, when it should have been about twice as long for most drivers. I can easily imagine a young Robbie Burns (who lived thereabouts) trundling along those old tracks on his pony, as he sought his next poetic copulation, but I digress.

We did attempt to get the driver to slow down, but even so he seemed incapable of driving at speeds less than 80mph and we were all a little nervous, notwithstanding his undoubted skill at the wheel. One gets used to the more sedate speeds mandated on Canadian highways. Anyway, we got to our hotel in one piece and the rest of the trip went well.

The following week we did exactly the same thing except that, before we boarded our taxi, Glen asked the cabbie to keep somewhere near the speed limit. Our driver obviously did his best, for it took us a good five minutes longer to reach our destination. This translated to no less than 70mph with occasional spurts up to 100. So that evening we had a short conference as to how to keep our otherwise splendid driver to a reasonable speed. "I know" says Hez. "Next week we will ask him to take us on the scenic route to Prestwick'. That way will be through narrow country lanes for most of the journey and he will have to moderate his speed or kill us all". So, on the following week we politely told our driver that we were unfamiliar with that part of the world and would he please take us on a leisurely scenic tour, ending up at the hotel.

I haven't yet described the driver. He was of

medium height, balding, and about 60 years of age, but his most distinguishing feature was his lack of teeth. Whether his whalleys were at the menders I do not know, but he spoke very quickly in what sounded like a foreign tongue, but was in fact standard received Glaswegian, the delivery of which was not helped by his lack of teeth.

Anyway, the following week we asked him to take us on the scenic route and he appeared absolutely delighted to oblige. Perhaps he was a frustrated tour-bus driver, for as soon as we set off, he launched into a nonstop commentary at about one hundred and twenty words a minute. Our seating in the cab was in strict accordance with seniority, which meant that poor old Hez was in the front seat, and therefore a micro second closer to death than were we. This meant that our driver appeared to be addressing most of his non-stop commentary to Hez, who couldn't understand a bloody word. He made up for this by faking a look of cognizance; at the same time nodding in what he hoped were the right places. Every now and then, Hez turned round to us with a shrug of total bewilderment. Luckily for me, and to some extent Glen (whose ancestry was roughly in that area), I could understand about half of what was being said, so it was not a totally lost cause. In any case, the purpose of the ruse was satisfied, for the journey took well over an hour, and two of us at least learnt something of that area of Scotland. I was pleased to meet Hez not too many months ago and among his own treasured memories is that journey from Glasgow Airport to Prestwick.

Apocrypha from the Sub Continent

There is a tale of a Qantas pilot who, on the approach to Bombay airport, replied to all air traffic transmissions in his personal version of the Indian accent. The conversation went something like this:

Pilot: "Bombay control, a very very good evening to you sir, this is Qantas 123 over the Bravo beacon inbound Heading 120"

Controller: (in his normal lilting Indian accent) "Qantas 123, I have you on radar, please turn on to Heading 085 and descend to 3000 feet, change to frequency 121.6".

Pilot: "Oh-h very very good, ve are going to 121.6 and wishing you a splendid good evening".

Changes to frequency 121.6. "Bombay tower this is Qantas 123 inbound on a heading of 085, altitude 3000feet".

Tower controller: " Good evening Qantas, please turn to heading 070 to intercept the ILS (Instrument Landing System) for runway 12. On interception you are clear for the approach; report at the outer marker"

Pilot (in his psuedo Bombay Welsh accent with the occasional momentary lapse into Standard Received Sydney): "Oh dear, very splendid sir, we will be delighted to comply with your wishes and will indeed report at the outer marker".

Controller (with just a hint of irritation in his voice): "Okay Qantas, and remain on this frequency".

The pilots carry out the procedure and 6 minutes later the aeroplane is on its final approach to runway 12 and over the outer marker beacon.

Pilot.: "Bombay tower, this is Qantas 123, outer marker inbound."

Controller: "Qantas 123 okay, you are clear to land".

Pilot: "Oh Thank you so very very much, ve understand ve are clear to land".

Controller: " Yes affirmative, you are clear to land, -------- and Qantas 123?"

Pilot: "Go ahead tower".

Controller: "and on arrival at the terminal I shall be meeting your aircraft --- and you'd better be an Indian!!

---------- and Mooshrooms!

My first flight to Manchester, England, was some time in the 1970's and among the passengers on that flight was a choir comprised of about fifty young people about to embark on a tour of Britain. Those were carefree days, and passengers were quite often allowed to visit the flight deck if they so requested, and if we were not having a "busy spell". Naturally, many of the young choristers wished to have a look at the sharp end and we cheerfully complied. I think just about the whole choir visited us during that flight, although we limited visitors to about three at any one time. They were all very friendly and cheerful, which no doubt augured well for their forthcoming tour. We did our best to explain that, yes, there were a lot of switches and dials and, yes, we did know a fair number of them. (A bit of exaggeration was called for).

It was, as usual, an overnight flight and we arrived at Manchester's Ringway airport at about 7am. In those days terminal buildings were often located some distance from the aircraft parking areas. Passengers were taken by bus to the main airport building. The usual procedure was that after deplaning, the passengers walked a few steps to board the waiting bus. However, the members of the choir ignored the bus altogether, formed up in three rows at the front of the aeroplane, and in full view of the cockpit. At a signal from their conductor we were then treated to an impromptu performance lasting about ten minutes. What an unconventional but delightful way of thanking us for an enjoyable flight. Perhaps some of them still have pleasant memories of a chilly morning of long ago when they entertained the crew of the DC8 that safely delivered them to Manchester.

We were due to fly the aeroplane up to Prestwick before calling it a day (or was it a night?), but had a couple of hours to wait whilst the aircraft was refueled and serviced. There were a few huts nearby and closer inspection revealed the workers' canteen. It was open, so we thought it a good idea to have breakfast while we were waiting. The canteen staff comprised three cheerful ladies, who, as is common in the North of England, freely used the word "Loov" when addressing us. We asked what was on the menu, to which one of the ladies responded in her strong Lancashire accent, "We cook a loovely breakfast. You can 'ave eggs, - and bacon, -and fried potatoes, -and beans, -and fried tomatoes, -and black pudding". This definitely held the promise that our fast would irrevocably be broken, and then her colleague quickly reminded her that the prospective frying pan was not yet full, for to my amusement she exclaimed "------- and Mooshrooms".

It is incidents such as these, sometimes lasting just a few seconds, which form so many of the treasured memories that continue to amuse us through the years. After relating this little tale to my wife, whenever a fry-up was planned for breakfast, one of us would inquire "--- and Mooshrooms?"

Exotic Cuisine

In order for passengers entering the Douglas DC8 to get to their assigned seats they had to pass by the aeroplane galley, often at the same time as provisions were in the final process of being boarded through the galley door and stowed in the food cabinets. The customers rarely got a look at what was in store for them at dinner time, but as the title of this book suggests there was a high probability that chicken and beef featured large on the menu. For passengers boarding at the Caribbean airports they could get a bit of a surprise if they peeped galleywards, for there on a shelf would be a couple of liquid containers labelled "Pilots Milk". Next to these would be a package on which was printed in large letters "Navigator Sandwiches". Very few of the cabin staff could see anything amusing in these two items of nourishment, but my warped sense of humour imagined somewhere among the sugar-cane fields a pasture on which navigators were being fattened before being slaughtered for the benefit of Air Canada passengers. Not far away from them would be a herd of pilots chewing the cud waiting patiently for milking time. -- An amusing mental picture, but not necessarily a pretty one.

Sadly the explanation is far less interesting. It seems that on the Caribbean runs some years previously, when one or more operating crew requested a glass of milk he was quite often informed that it was in short supply, and the customers came first. The union representative whose job it was to monitor these problems fought a successful campaign to have some dedicated containers of milk boarded for the exclusive use of the pilots (and navigator if there was one). I suppose they could have labelled them "Milk for Pilots use only" or "Cabin Staff keep yer sticky 'ands orff", or some such inscription, and I think that "Pilots Milk" was a bit saucy.

As a navigator working on the outer Caribbean routes I did not find the task of keeping the aeroplane on the assigned course particularly demanding of my skill, and I could certainly find time to consume the occasional morsel that came from the rich man's table in First Class. I could even throw caution to the wind and have a natter with the lass who had the goodness of heart to think of the dear old Nav. Some of my colleagues did not share this insouciant attitude towards navigating over the high seas, and one in particular found the job so demanding that it took all his skill and concentration, with no time to relax. His modus operandi was to surround the flight-navigator station with the night curtain and toil non-stop within this tent. He made it plain that interruptions be for operational purposes only, and please, no idle chat. He certainly could not cope with a meal tray, or deal with knives and forks as well as his HB pencil. However, like all of us he did get hungry. He must have put the problem to higher authority, probably the Chief Navigator, for before long a message went out to all stations that they were to prepare for the navigator a separate pack of sandwiches – and there you have it -- Navigator Sandwiches. So to those passengers who may have glimpsed these items as standing on the galley counter, Air Canada did not indulge in cannibalism. Of course, we now have female pilots, which could give a whole different meaning to "Pilots Milk".

Cock-Ups in the Catering Department

The title of this little book is very much a response to my experience over many years of airline cuisine. It seems that chicken and beef have proved to be the safest and easiest way to cater for the necessity to give the customers some nourishment on longer journeys. However, to cater for the brethren of other faiths, there *are* alternatives to these two basic meats. There is in place a system where, if one's dietary intake is governed by the will of Allah, or the chosen representatives of some other deity, then a quick phone call in good time before the flight will ensure that a "special meal" will be available about two hours after take-off. When the flight attendants start rushing up and down the aisles, the air around them redolent with Eastern Spices, the infidels among us know that, before too long, our own feast will be plonked on our little table.

A good friend of mine decided that he was fed up with being given a lump of white chicken or a piece of braised mystery meat on his crew meal-tray, so he decided to become a vegetarian during working hours. This little ruse enabled him to enjoy something a bit different – perhaps a nut cutlet, or a soy filled cabbage roll (ugh!), as he winged his way around the globe. I can well remember a significant delay at Paris De Gaulle airport as one of the ground agents floundered around trying to find the First Officer's special meal. I happened to be on the adjacent aeroplane awaiting departure, so I piped up on the radio "'Allo Don, nice Wiener Schnitzel we had last night, wasn't it?"

As I say, 'Chicken or Beef' seem to be the meats of choice for airline catering departments. Occasionally they provide other alternatives, but these seem to be fraught with potential hazards as to taste and toxicity. I well remember an urgent radio call to an aircraft already winging its way to London. The gist of the message was "On no account give the passengers (and hopefully by implication, the crew) the fish." There has been at least one Japanese airline chef who committed Hara-kiri after some customers enjoyed their last meal whilst on board one of the company's aircraft.

It is not all doom and gloom, and sometimes the beef or the chicken can be very tasty and passengers have no reason to complain. In any case, the company often adds fish to the choices, as well as very occasionally, lamb. For some reason they never seem to have pork, although surely those who would object to it would already be treated as "special needs" customers.

In the early eighties, I was drafted to fly a DC8 from Vancouver to Calgary and thence to Toronto. The captain was a short fellow who made up for his lack of height with an impressive girth. He clearly enjoyed his food – any food – and his prodigious appetite was rarely satisfied with just a standard crew meal.

We understood that this particular flight would be without customers from Vancouver to Calgary, but have a full load of about two hundred passengers leaving Calgary. In fact, it was the opposite, with not a single passenger or flight attendant from Calgary to Toronto..

The catering department had got the same information as we had, and therefore catered for a full load for the four-hour flight to Toronto: - two hundred meals, half of which were chicken and the rest lamb chops, two on each tray, a total of two hundred lamb cutlets, two hundred little pat of butter, the same number of little pieces of wrapped cheese etc., and so forth – and not a single customer. Food safety regulations would decree that all this 'luverly grub' would be trashed on arrival at Toronto (if the Toronto ground staff did not filch it - and who can blame them?).

Well, old Fred (the captain) thought he had gone to heaven. As soon after take-off that he could safely leave the flight deck, he disappeared through the crew door. He was back in his seat about fifteen minutes later with a tray loaded with seven lamb chops, copious quantities of veggies, and about 6 pieces of cheese, as well as two desserts and a large glass of juice. It was a joy to behold to see him tucking into this prodigious repast, and when it was over all that remained was a look of gastronomic content. I could not risk leaving my crew position until our good old captain had completed his impressive repast, for an unexpected violent manoevre (it's been known to happen) would have resulted in lamb chops, mashed potatoes and peas flying in all directions. (The standard response to an unexpected emergency whilst eating one's meal, is to throw the loaded tray backwards, away from the controls and instruments).

Anyway, as soon as I could safely leave, I made my way to the galley and delved through the ovens, coming away with a modest four chops and some veggies. I also found a plastic bag into which went about a pound of cheese, which would eventually find its way to the Deere fridge at home, and subsequently into the mouths of babes (mine). As far as I can remember, that was the only major catering cock-up in which I was a beneficiary of sorts. Mostly it was small failures in which the crew meals were not on board, or there was a shortage of chicken or beef in favour of chicken or beef, so to speak. All in all, our company did a splendid job of feeding the madding crowd, and was very often in the top five airlines when it came to passenger satisfaction.

Finis

It was on the 31st Day of March of the year dot, and I was flying for the very last time as an airline pilot. My sixtieth birthday had occurred just four days before and the rules stated that one could not fly as a pilot beyond midnight on the last day of the month of one's sixtieth birthday. So this was "it" -- almost forty years since I first climbed into the open cockpit of a De-Haviland Tiger Moth biplane for my first flying lesson.

Ed, the captain, had kindly allowed me to be the PF (Pilot Flying as opposed to PNF - pilot not flying) for the four flight legs to Kingston, Jamaica and return and we were now on the approach to Toronto Airport. From about 3000 feet above ground we had been in cloud, the base of which was reported to be 200 feet, the minimum for the approach procedure for that runway. At 1700 feet we reported at the outer marker beacon, I called for 25 degrees of flap and reduced the airspeed to the proper approach speed. The Air Traffic Controller gave us clearance to land. From that point on we followed the glide slope at a descent rate of 700 feet per minute. At the appropriate point, Ed called "100 feet above". We were exactly on glide path and speed. The next call was "Minimum, runway in sight" I looked up from the instruments and there ahead were the approach lights with the runway lights in two parallel lines beyond. At the appropriate point, Ed called "50 feet", the signal for me to ease back slightly on the control column, and the aircraft arrived on the hard surface with just a gentle thump. We taxied to the arrival gate, stopped the engines and completed the shut down procedures. The end of a career.

I climbed from my seat for the last time, hauled my flight bag from its stowage, then donned my jacket and put on my cap. Ed was kind enough to take a few commemorative photos, and it was all over. As I left the flight deck for the last time I took a backward glance to be sure nothing was left behind --- certainly not my memories.

Final thoughts

Well, I am at the end of this brief journey through some of the lighter moments of my second career. I have derived considerable satisfaction in putting them down on paper. If you, the reader, have stayed the course you have my gratitude, for without an audience our anecdotes die on the vine. Hopefully you have been rewarded with a chuckle or two. Please remember when you are next sitting in "Hostility Class" that you are in very good hands, and that is due in no small part to the rigorous training and personal qualities of those fellows at the sharp end -- and yes, as I hope I have shown, they do possess a sense of humour. But remember to be ready for the stewardess as she wheels the trolley down the aisle -- will you be having "Chicken or Beef?"